S E P I

R I S E O F

ORLANDO SANCHEZ

Other titles by Orlando Sanchez

The Spiritual Warriors

Blur-A John Kane Novel

The Deepest Cut-A Blur Short

The Last Dance-A Sepia Blue Short

SEPIA BLUE-Rise of the Night

Copyright © 2014 by Orlando Sanchez.

OM Publishing NY, NY

For information contact: www.nascentnovels.com

Book and Cover design by RexDesign Inc.

Cover images used by permission of Shutterstock

ISBN-13:978-1499554229
ISBN-10:1499554222
First Edition: May 2014

10 9 8 7 6 5 4 3 2 1

ACKNOWLEDGEMENTS

Every book is a group effort. So let me take a moment to acknowledge my (very large) group:

To Dolly: my wife and biggest fan. You make all of this possible and keep me grounded, especially when I get into my writing to the exclusion of everything else. Thank you, I love you.

To my Tribe: You are the reason I have stories to tell. You cannot possibly fathom how much and how deep I love you all.

To Lee: Because you were the first audience I ever had. I love you sis.

To my editor Lorelei: This was my first time putting a book in the hands of a professional editor. It was a nerve wracking and exciting experience all at once. It was an excellent learning experience. I learned I still have far to go as a writer, thank you Lorelei. I also learned, third person present- not so much fun. I don't have the words to thank you for your amazing work. Your thoughts and comments made this story go from good to great. Any mistakes in the story are mine.

To you the reader: Thank you for getting on this ride with me. I truly hope you enjoy this story. You are the reason I wrote it.

ONE

HER BODY SLAMMED into the wall, cracking brick and ribs. Brick dust covered her jet black hair and filled her eyes, temporarily blinding her. The impact forced the breath from her body in a violent gasp.

Shit, that hurts.

Spots danced on the edge of her vision and the dust coated her lips as she inhaled. Heat flushed her body the next moment as she felt her ink flare, muting the pain, knitting bone and tissue. The meaty hand around her neck began to squeeze. Part of her brain realized that this was a very bad situation, but she ignored it. *Always stating the obvious,* she thought as her vision began to tunnel in. Taking a moment to orient herself, she looked up the arm of the mountain that just threatened to crush her into a wall. He bared his teeth in what she could only imagine was a smile. Brutes were not known for their intelligence. They were big, strong, fast, and almost impossible to kill. She was glad there was only one.

"I have a clear shot," said the voice over her comlink.

She shook her head side to side hoping her gunman would understand the signal not to shoot. With her remaining breath she planted her feet against the wall and pushed, forcing the brute to step back and loosen his grip for a second. A second was all she needed as she reached up, pulled back on his hand and broke the thumb, compromising the stranglehold around her neck. It was so sudden the brute was confused by her escape and looked at his hand, bewildered. Cade cursed under his breath in her ear.

"Sepia, let me end him. He didn't even feel that, the bastard." She crouched under the haymaker that would have removed her head from her body had it connected.

"I need information, Cade. I can't get it if it's dead.

"Better it than you."

"No killing." She rolled behind the brute as it delivered a stomp that shattered the wall behind her. This was turning into a bad night. She needed to take this thing down without killing it, and she wasn't seeing a way to do it. She turned to the brute as it advanced.

"If you tell me why you are so far from home, I promise not to kill you," she said. She didn't expect a response; brutes didn't have a formal language or the power of speech, just destruction.

"Hunter dies tonight." The brute's voice was a rasp. The words, the grinding of two boulders, all jagged edges and pain.

"What the fu-" Cade was mid-sentence when a head shot took down the brute. There was a look of shock mixed with surprise on the brute's face. It took one more step before crashing to the ground.

"Goddammit, Cade, I told you no killing!" She rolled the brute over to check the body, finding nothing of importance. *What is it doing so far downtown? Who sent it? Did it really just speak to me? Could the Unholy be intelligent? Too many unanswered questions.*

"That wasn't me, and since when did they learn to speak? I've never heard one of them speak, ever," said Cade.

She turned, scanning the rooftops as she answered.

"Me either, I didn't even think brutes were capable of language. He is clear on the message though. Someone wants me dead," said Sepia. "It means we have a shadow."

She knew Cade well enough to know he would never kill unless she was in real danger. No, this was someone else. Someone was trying to make a point.

"Let's see how good they are, Cade"

"I'm already moving."

"Meet you there."

She had a rough idea of where the shooter would have set up judging from the trajectory of the shot. She ran toward the building she thought the sniper has used. The streets in lower New York were a labyrinth, thanks to the English, which made finding the right building a challenge. She reached the rooftop at the same time as Cade scaled over the opposite edge.

"Whoever they are, they're good. That's easily a four hundred-yard shot," said Cade as he paced around the roof taking in vantage points. Sepia shook the brick dust out of her hair revealing the white shock that had been with her since her late twenties.

"Good, but good as you? How many gunners can make that shot, you think?" Sepia looked over the edge of the roof trying to gauge how high up they were.

"We're about forty feet up. How many? All of them. At least all the ones I know."

Cade was crouched over the edge, where he saw a small impression in the slate. He rubbed his fingers in it.

"He took the shot from here. Not bad. Far enough to be difficult but close enough to hide," said Cade

"This smells all kinds of wrong," she said.

"If you had let me take my shot--" he started. Sepia glared at him.

"Sepia, you can't keep doing this. These principles or ideals or whatever you want to call them are going to get us killed. You have to eliminate the Unholy. It's the only way you get to go home at the end of your tour. You know I'm right."

He towered over her as he spoke, looking every part the ex-military man he was. His close-cropped black hair shot through with gray only added to the image.

"No, all life is sacred--even unholy life," she said.

"Then you are in the wrong line of work, Blue. I am sure they don't feel the same way you do."

"Don't go all drill sergeant on me, you know it doesn't work, never has," she said as she stood on the edge of the building.

"I'm just saying this position of yours,--" he started

"We do this my way. No killing," she said and jumped off the side of the building, executing a flip midair before the deserted street swallowed her footsteps as she walked away.

TWO

SHE HATED WHEN he was right. She trained hard, harder than any other Hunter. Just so she didn't have to kill. Every night that she went out on tour, she took her life into her hands. All she had ever wanted was a normal life. She was so far from normal at this point, she didn't know what the word meant. She knew Cade was trailing her close by. He always gave her space after a fight. As partners went, he was one of the best. At least he wasn't trigger happy like her last partner. She shuddered at the memory of patrolling with Ronin. The body counts were so high, each night felt like a massacre. She was different back then. Everyone said they were an effective team; right up to the moment he tried to kill her. *Was that really two years ago?*

That was a memory better left in the past. *Could he be the sniper? No, Ronin is long gone. I made sure of that.* As a class two Hunter she was responsible for a sector in the lower region of Manhattan--from 14th street to the tip of the island, east and west sides. The island was divided into ten regions, each region divided into smaller sectors with hers being one of the smaller ones. Every area of Manhattan was covered by a hunter and her gunman. Each night, thousands of pairs patrolled the city against the Unholy. Every region was under the Order's jurisdiction, except Central Park. The wards around it declared it off-limits to hunters and the Order. Hunters didn't go in the park, not if they liked breathing. The Unholy stayed in the park. It was a centuries-old agreement enforced by the wards and established to maintain balance. If you entered the park, you did so at your own risk. No one could or would save you if the Unholy found you there.

Cade's voice came in on her com. "Hey, we have some activity over here."

"Where?"

"About half a click from my position," said Cade.

"You know I hate the whole GPS thing."

"One of the abilities of a hunter is to know where her gunman is at all times," said Cade, sounding like a textbook. "Said ability is to be honed and perfected until said hunter can locate her gunman within one yard of any location."

"I hate you."

"I know, now hurry your ass over here."

Sepia took a deep breath and turned in a circle until she could feel the specific vibration that was Cade.

"Got you," she said.

"Make sure. Remember what happened the last time you thought you located me."

"That was a mistake. How would I know you have the same vibrational frequency as an orangutan?"

"I don't. You have no skill at geolocation. I'm moving in to get a better look."

"I see you—wait, what the hell is that?"

Sepia made out Cade's silhouette on the adjacent roof. As she drew closer the pressure in the air felt like a weight on her chest making it hard to breathe.

"By all that's holy-- we need back up. Call Home. Call them now," he said.

"It can't be, Cade, that feels like a-"

"It's a Nightmare," said Cade.

THREE

"A WHAT? WHERE? That is impossible, Miss Blue. There are wards and barriers around the park to prevent this sort of incident," said the female voice over her com.

"I know what I am sensing and that is a Nightmare. Get some Rogues here, now," said Sepia. She and Cade were both lying down on the roof, careful not to look over the edge.

"Very well, you have two Rogues incoming. Call me back with a status report."

"How many Rogues coming? Twenty, Thirty?"

"We must be short on Rogues. They're sending two," said Sepia

"How can we be short on them? They have no patrols and we basically use them as shock troops. Are you sure you heard right? Maybe she meant two dozen?"

"Two, Cade. Two, as in one, two," said Sepia.

"Did you mention it was a Nightmare?"

"Cade."

"Fine, fine, what are we going to do with two rogues? Feed that thing? It's going to take a lot more than the four of us to take that thing down." *Not if I use my sword,* she thought. Cade looked over the edge of the roof to where the Nightmare was standing on the street below.

"What T level do you think it is?" Cade said as he looked over the edge of the roof again.

"I haven't heard of a Nightmare lower than a threat level four," said Sepia.

As Cade looked, the Nightmare grabbed a woman from the sidewalk and embraced her in his arms. She struggled for a moment, before it was too late. As he began to kiss her, Cade could see her skin wither away. The Nightmare kept her in his arms until she was dust, having absorbed every bit of moisture from her body, down to the marrow. What remained of her blew away.

"It's a drinker. This is going to be a bitch," said Cade. "Those things are worse than brutes."

"How the hell did it get out of the park and what is it doing here?" she said.

"Both good questions. Why don't you go down there and ask him?" said Cade. "I think I hear our back up." He propped his rifle on the edge, calculating a firing solution.

A motorcycle carrying two riders was screaming down the street.

"It's time to join the party," said Sepia.

She jumped across to the roof opposite hers and slid down to the street below to intercept the motorcycle before it drove into the Nightmare. The motorcycle came to a screeching stop as the rider braked and slid. Sepia walked over to the motorcycle.

"Who the hell are you?" She looked at the two riders and moved to adjust her glasses, which were missing.

"Goddammit Cade, where are my glasses?"

The anger crept into her voice and fear joined it. *These two are going to die tonight,* she thought.

"We are your back up, Miss Blue. Let's do this!" said the passenger of the motorcycle.

"Dead men walking is what they are. They just don't know it yet," said Cade over her com.

"What's your name?" said Sepia as she pointed at the driver.

"Frank, Miss Blue. I'm Frank Mannoli. This here is Greg, my partner and little brother. Frank elbowed Greg as the latter stared at Sepia. She could see the resemblance. Greg was a younger version of his big brother, and still full of hero worship it seemed.

"Sorry, Miss Blue, he's kind of new," said Frank.

Sepia was used to this. She knew her features unsettled those who met her.

"Okay let's get this out of the way so we have no distractions later, you know, when we're trying to stay alive," she said.

The motorcycle headlight shone directly on her, and judging from the look on Greg's face she knew what she must look like to him.

She planted a foot on the front wheel of the bike. The soft leather she wore creaked as she adjusted her boot straps.

"You two ever face a Nightmare?"

Sepia looked at them and could smell the fear. Greg shook his head no.

"Once, as a trainee, and we barely escaped alive. Out of ten of us only three made it back," said Frank.

Greg visibly blanched. *What is Home thinking sending her two rookies to face a Nightmare?*

"Fine, we play this my way. You have a problem with that you may as well leave right now. Are we clear?" Frank and Greg nodded.

"Did you find your glasses? Oh hell, you didn't. No wonder the kid wants to pee his pants," said Cade.

Sepia pulled her hair back and tied it into a ponytail. Her shock of white escaped and fell across her face before she managed to get it under control.

"See this?" She pointed at her hair. "A T4 Lifestealer decided I no longer needed to live, and tried to siphon my life. I disagreed. I had to kill it."

She let the words hang in the air. She knew the Nightmare deserved it. That didn't make it any easier.

"When it comes down to it, it will always be a choice between your life and theirs," said Sepia.

She would choose hers every time. Sacrifice, she could live with, self-sacrifice, not so much, literally.

She was checking her guns while she spoke: twin revolvers, custom made to hold eight rounds of explosive ammunition.

Frank and Greg checked their guns as well, aware of the fact that she felt self-conscious talking about herself.

"Is that what happened to your eye too, Miss Blue?" Greg blurted. She could hear Cade laughing.

"Serves you right for scaring the kid," said Cade.

Frank groaned and rolled his eyes.

"No, Greg, the eye was a gift from my mother on the day she died. It's one of the reasons I'm a hunter," said Sepia.

"Nightmare is on the move," interrupted Cade.

"Let's go crash this party. I want you two to go left one block and down for ten then come back and flank it. I will try the more direct approach." *Twenty blocks and one avenue is hopefully enough time to deal with this thing before they engage, and die.*

Frank started the motorcycle. Greg jumped on the back. He looked back and gave Sepia a thumb up.

He must think this is some adventure. Was I ever that green? When she sees them turn the corner she headed toward the Nightmare at a jog.

"There is no flanking a Nightmare, Blue. Trying to get rid of them?" Cade whispered in her ear.

"Trying to keep them alive, at least for tonight," replied Sepia.

"You rigged the bike."

"Cade, did you see the kid? He would last exactly ten seconds against a T2 and this has to be at least a T4. Might as well shoot him myself and call it a night."

She ran down the street to confront the Nightmare, calculating that in about three minutes the front tire would deflate from a small explosive placed there. It would keep the Rogues away from the fight long enough for her to end it. She hoped.

The Nightmare turned to face her. Unlike the brutes, the Nightmares were intelligent and ruthless. The Threat scale was based on interactions with these creatures. They thrived on fear and destruction. Like the brutes, they were incredibly hard to kill.

"Just in time, hunter, I'm thirsty," said the Nightmare.

FOUR

SEPIA BEGAN TO SHOOT. The Nightmare leapt behind a car, as he shot projectiles from his hands at Sepia forcing her to duck behind the cover of an SUV.

Black globules punctured and penetrated the vehicle. She could hear the metal of the car sizzle and melt like bacon fat on a hot skillet.

"That's just rude," the Nightmare shouted from behind the cover of the car.

"Show your face and I'll show you how rude I can be." She checked herself to make sure none of the projectiles had hit.

"Cade, do you have a shot? I don't want to get much closer than I have to. That thing is shooting some kind of metal-eating acid."

"I have no shot, and he knows our MO. Can you flush him out?"

She hated the idea of using her sword, but she didn't have the luxury of time, since any minute those two Rogues would be back and then all hell would break loose.

"Let me see if I can convince him to move," said Cade. "You're going to have to dance with him, though. I don't think my ammo is going to do much to him. I hate Nightmares."

She knew what that meant. She would have to draw it, her sword. *Where is a shadow sniper when you need one?*

"Do what you can, we don't have all night. Those two will hoof it back eventually," she said.

The first shot shattered the windshield of the car where the Nightmare was hiding. Cade could see the car being slowly lifted.

"Get the hell out of there, now!" he yelled.

Sepia dove and rolled into the street as the SUV she was taking cover behind was crushed.

"That is not a T4, Blue. Get the hell out of there--bug out!

"Too late now," she said.

As she stood, Sepia could see the Nightmare was close, too close.

"I'm going to drink you slowly, bitch," said the Nightmare with a smile.

Its voice was silk, warm and inviting. It was a gentle caress with the promise of death.

"I can see you heal fast," responded Sepia.

The only evidence of the bullets she fired was a series of small puckers now, healing fast.

"We aren't as frail as humans, hunter. We don't die from bullets."

Shooting them did slow them down, which is all a hunter needed when seconds mattered.

"I know, I just wanted your attention," said Sepia.

She drew her sword and a hush fell on the street, the night holding its breath for a moment and then exhaling. She leapt forward, slicing fast. The Nightmare was faster. Her first lunge missed and she avoided his swipe by a fraction of an inch.

Damn, it's fast.

"You're good, hunter," it said as it circled around her. "I'm going to enjoy you, and your partner up there in the shadows, will be dessert."

Cade is right, it knows how we operate, but how?

"What are you doing out of the park?" she said as she looked for an opening.

"Wouldn't you like to know? More importantly, wouldn't you like to know how?"

The Nightmare slid left, extending its hand and firing projectiles at her. She dodged right avoiding the black globules and slashed in an upward arc from left to right. Her sword connected with the Nightmare and she felt the surge of power. Her sword loved this. The darkness rose in her.

The Nightmare looked down to see a huge gash open across its chest. Sepia stood transfixed. *How is this thing not down yet?* It feinted right and jumped left slamming a palm in her chest. She flowed with the energy of the strike, allowing her body to turn and slash to remove the Nightmare's head. It ducked under the slash and kicked at her feet. She leapt to avoid the sweep and realized her mistake too late. The voice of her swordmaster came back to her. *Never leave the ground with both feet while fighting something faster and stronger than you unless you are jumping off a building.* Gan would kick her ass for this amateur hour move.

The Nightmare now crouched, jumped up with a knee strike that connected with her midsection, doubling her over. The pain was intense as she staggered back, retching.

"Sepia! Sepia, you okay? Bastard knows I'm here and is blocking my shot," said Cade. "I'm moving for better position."

She could see how the Nightmare blocked Cade's line of sight using the building as a barrier. It turned to face her. The gash across its chest was gone.

"I'm not impressed, frankly. I heard hunters were supposed to be this fearsome group of individuals. I can see the reports of your abilities were greatly exaggerated."

"You leave her alone!" yelled Greg. Charging behind the Nightmare, he began shooting.

The shots rang out in the night. *The weapon isn't even silenced?* Sepia realized. The Nightmare took several steps forward from the impact. It was the only indicator that it had been shot several times. The lack of exit wounds meant that whatever weapon Greg was using was underpowered. She could see Frank trailing in the distance. *I underestimated the Nightmare and took too long, and now this boy will die.*

"Greg, no, stay back! It's too dangerous," she said as she managed to get some air back into her lungs. The Nightmare spun and grabbed Greg by the neck, suspending him several feet from the ground.

"See, this is what I mean hunter. This is insulting. How could your superiors send this against a creature of my caliber?" *My thoughts exactly. Goddammit, kid. I told you it was dangerous.* The Nightmare closed its grip and snapped Greg's neck, tossing the lifeless body to the ground.

"No!" screamed Frank.

Frank saw the body of his brother crumple to the ground. Cade managed to grab him before he attacked the Nightmare.

"You can't, buddy. It's too strong. Let her deal with it," said Cade.

"That was my brother, my little brother," said Frank as he choked back the sobs.

"If you want to be around to remember him, we need to put some distance between us and them Frank. Now move," said Cade.

Cade grabbed Frank and pulled him back. The Nightmare turned to face Sepia again.

"I hope he wasn't important to you, hunter, though you are all so…insignificant."

Sepia stood still, the anger coursing through her body coming off her in palpable waves. The darkness flowed now. She hated this life, she hated this job and she hated the senseless death. This creature, this thing killed indiscriminately, leaving a wake of destruction behind it. No more.

Her sword hummed with power as she jumped at the Nightmare. Covered with a dark aura, it crackled with energy. The blade had gone black, an inky viscous ooze covering it.

"What the hell is that?" said Frank. He pointed at Sepia's sword.

"Yeah, we'd better move back a bit more," said Cade as he grabbed Frank's arm.

"What is that? What happened to her sword? Why is it black like that?"

"That's a named blade, which means right now that Nightmare doesn't know it's in for a world of hurt."

"A named blade?" said Frank.

"Don't you guys get briefed?" Cade said as they were still moving away from Sepia and the Nightmare. "Goddamned rookies. Named blades are given to certain hunters, the most dangerous ones. All you need to know is that right now we are moving away from *her*, not the Nightmare."

The Nightmare dodged another slash and sidestepped right into a kick. Sepia shattered its left knee as it fell to the ground. She slashed downward, and the Nightmare lifted an arm to intercept the strike, so she changed direction mid strike and turned her wrist in a J motion and removed the Nightmare's arm. Shock registered on its face. For the first time, the Nightmare knew fear. Its knee already healed, it stood to run.

"Where are you going? I thought you wanted to drink me dry?" she whispered as she kicked the arm away, making sure it didn't join its host.

"I've decided to try a different vintage tonight. I'm finding the selection here is quite bitter to my palate."

"Oh, I'm not bitter; I'm as sweet as they come. Let me show you."

She feinted right and stabbed left. Impaled, the light of realization dawned in the Nightmare's eyes as he looked down to see her sword in its chest. She removed the sword and the Nightmare fell to its knees. There was a smile on her face now. It was visceral and twisted. She held the sword at her side looking down at the Nightmare.

"That sword- -is that Per-"

The Nightmare's head flew to the side before he could finish. She looked over to where the head rolled. The Nightmare disintegrated, the remaining dust blowing away. In a few minutes, no evidence of its existence would be left.

"You, filth, will not utter its name," she said as she sheathed her blade.

"Cade," she said as she took several steps, as the world tilted and she collapsed.

FIVE

"SHE IS A LIABILITY. What kind of hunter wields her sword and then passes out?"

Magnus Peterson was an imposing figure, taller than most all his life; he looked down at his second in command, Marks, as they walked the halls of Home to his office. As Overseer for the Order he was responsible for half the Hunters on the island. The other half were under the jurisdiction of Rebecca Wright, a hunter who rose through the ranks. It was his opinion that no woman should be an Overseer. They just weren't strong or ruthless enough. It was a job for a man, cold, calculating, and logical. He would rectify that mistake soon enough. Right now he had to deal with this mess.

"Who is patrolling her sector now?"

"I assigned Jen Rodriguez and Burns, sir," said Marks.

"Well, at least they're competent. I swear whoever thought women were capable of being hunters needs to be tied to a post and shot."

"Yes, sir," said Marks.

"Why don't we designate her as Rogue and replace her?"

"Policy states that no hunter can be demoted or leave their post for any reason, short of death, sir."

"It was a rhetorical question, Marks. Don't be dense. I know the regulations better than you ever will."

"Yes, sir."

They rounded a corner and proceeded down the corridor to an intersection, taking the right hallway as Magnus continued speaking.

Marks checked his tablet as they walked.

"However, it says here that she has one year left on her five year mandatory sector patrol. She is currently patrolling sector thirteen."

"Isn't that our smallest sector?"

"Yes, sir, and one of the farthest away from the park."

What is a Nightmare doing so far away from the park and why in that sector? There is something deeper here, thought Magnus.

"Were there any fatalities?"

"There were two, sir. One is collateral, eliminated by the Nightmare. The other fatality is a Rogue by the name of Greg Mannoli."

"Locate the family of the collateral and make sure they are well compensated and taken care of. No need for them to suffer any more because of the incompetence of our hunter."

"Yes, sir. Full honors for the Rogue?"

"Of course, standard protocol."

"Yes, sir."

"What was the threat level of this Nightmare?"

His division, a nexus of activity, skipped a beat as Magnus entered. He kept walking toward his office, appearing oblivious to the pause, but well aware of his effect on those around him.

"Marks, what was the threat level?"

Marks checked his tablet.

"According to the data gathered and the regenerative processes, it would seem she faced a threat level six Nightmare."

Magnus turned to face his assistant, stopping for the first time. He pushed open the door to his office and sat down at his desk.

"No hunter can take down a T6 by herself. You must be mistaken."

"That is a possibility, sir. Should I run the data again?"

"Get me the report in an hour. I want the details. Close the door on your way out."

Who the hell is this hunter and how is she able to handle a T6 on her own?

****

Sepia regained consciousness in the infirmary. Beside her sat Cade and her trainer and mentor, Gan.

"She can't keep doing this, Gan," said Cade.

"Doing what exactly? Surviving?"

Cade stood and looked out the window. It was morning, with people on their way to work living their lives. They started the day, oblivious to the danger that existed beside them contained by wards older than the city itself. Wards, that -if last night was any indicator-, were failing.

Cade turned to face Gan. The trainer looked older this morning somehow. Built like a fireplug, Gan was mostly muscle. His bald head softly reflected the morning light coming in through the window. Numerous scars crisscrossed his arms and hands, testament to his time in the field.

"Patrolling, Gan. You know damned well what I mean. She has what, a year left on her mandatory? Get her transferred."

"You know regs as well as I do. Not possible."

Gan sat with his arms crossed still looking at Sepia. His large frame filled the chair, his face unreadable.

"She is going to get herself killed, and me with her."

"Occupational hazard, you know the risks especially with a named blade hunter. You getting cold feet, now, five years in?"

"It's this principle of hers. All life is sacred--even the Unholy. You should hear her."

"I don't need to, I taught her." Gan's eyes narrowed as he looked at Cade.

"She is going to get us in too deep one day."

"Hasn't happened yet," said Gan

Cade ran his hand through his hair, a nervous tic.

"By all that's holy, Gan, one moment she won't take down a brute. The next she's facing a T6, alone! It's that goddamned sword. It's messing with her head."

Gan sighed and turned then. Cade knew he crossed a line.

"Three things." Gan's voice was steel, its edge slicing through the air.

"One, you do not raise your voice to me, ever. You haven't come close to earning that privilege."

"I'm sor--" started Cade.

"Don't interrupt me when I'm speaking," said Gan.

Cade winced.

"Second, she didn't take on the T6 alone. Your sorry ass was there to make sure she made it out alive. You were supposed to find a vantage point that allowed you a shot. That's your job isn't it, gunman?"

Cade knew better than to answer and so he nodded.

"Third, she is a class two hunter and carries a named blade for a reason. She is the first class two to ever carry one. Whether or not she chooses to use it is another matter. I trained her. If she weren't capable she wouldn't be out there."

Gan turned to face the window, his reflection a granite mask.

"I need some coffee, and then I'm heading home. It's been a long night," said Cade.

Gan grunted in response. Cade knew better than to push it.

"I'll check on the Rogue on my way out," said Cade.

If Gan heard him he gave no indication as he kept staring out the window. The door closed behind Cade with a whisper.

"I know you're awake so stop pretending," said Gan.

Sepia opened her eyes. She could never fool Gan. She held her hand to her head, avoiding the light coming in from the window.

"Hurts?"

"Like a bitch. Coffee would be great right about now," said Sepia.

Gan handed her a steaming cup, which she inhaled slowly before her first sip. She swung her legs over the edge of the bed, her feet dangling several inches from the floor. She felt small again. Ever since she could remember, Gan was there.

"When your mother named me your guardian, I thought she was just being foolish. Gunmen don't have long lives, and then she died. She was talented, Sepia, probably the best hunter I have ever seen. A T8 took her down, because she faced it alone."

"I know, Gan," said Sepia

"No, no you don't, I was there. The sword you carry is hers. Are you tired of living?"

"No, Gan, I just--"

Gan held up his hand, stopping her answer.

"You can't suppress that sword and expect nothing to happen. You have to use it. It's like a pipe under pressure, and every so often you have to vent the line."

She looked down at her feet.

"I can't, Gan, every time I draw that thing it changes me, for the worse. It feels wrong, evil."

Gan knew firsthand what she was referring to. Her mother had said the same thing many times. But Sepia had to learn to use her sword, because the alternative was unthinkable.

"Get dressed. We have somewhere to go," said Gan.

"Is Cade…?"

"Pissed as hell? Yes. That other rogue is fine, and his brother was put to rest."

Another death I am responsible for. How much longer? How many more?

"Stop that. It isn't your fault, they are Rogues, and they knew what they were signing up for. Cut the sympathy shit, you can't afford it."

Sepia nodded as she started getting dressed.

"I'll be outside, make it quick," said Gan.

SIX

SEPIA PUT ON HER LEATHERS, tied her holsters and stepped out of the room. Gan handed her weapons over as they headed out of the infirmary.

"Where are we going?"

She holstered her guns. The sword was in its sheath. She strapped it to her back, its weight familiar, like an old friend.

24

"You need to find out what a T6 is doing in your sector. I think I know someone who can help you," said Gan

"Gan?" she said, concern in her voice.

"I'm not going out into the field with you. Heaven knows you need the help, though. No, I'm just pointing you in the right direction. You and Cade do the legwork."

"Right, this isn't you in the field," she said.

They were outside the Home site walking down Fifth Avenue from 82nd Street.

"This is you and I taking a walk and visiting an old friend of mine," he said as he raised his hand to hail a cab, which stopped a few feet in front of them.

"Downtown, 23rd and Madison, I'll show you the house when we get there," Gan said to the driver. As they drove down, Sepia took in the sights of her city. Sepia loved and hated her city. She couldn't see herself living anywhere else. The city was alive and vibrant during the day, and cold and hard during the night. It understood her and she understood it. They were made for each other. They made good time as the driver turned on to 23rd Street.

"You can leave us here," said Gan.

Gan paid the driver and the taxi drove off as they stood before the address he had given the driver.

"I hope she hasn't moved. She always said she wanted to live in the country," said Gan.

"Who, Gan? Wait a minute-- you don't even know if she still lives in the city?"

Gan waved his hand, dismissing her comment. He proceeded to walk ahead of her as she shook her head in disbelief. They crossed the street and headed up Madison Avenue. On 26th Street they made a left and Gan slowed his pace.

"I thought the place is on 23rd?"

Gan gave her a withering stare. "Tell me I trained you better than that."

He turned his back on her and kept walking down the street.

"There, the gray townhouse," he said as he pointed at an ornate townhouse that was several stories taller than its neighbors.

"Who lives here, Gan?" Sepia said with unease. She didn't like the feeling she was getting from the house. It felt as if the sidewalk was electrified, and each step sent small jolts into her feet as she drew closer.

"Calisto lives here, or at least she used to," said Gan as they stopped in front of the house.

"Calisto? You mean Calisto the witch? The one who has a standing kill order on her from the Order? *That* Calisto?"

Gan smiled at Sepia and spread his arms.

"This is as far as I go, so you'd better hurry. Her place moves around every thirty minutes or so, last I remember," he said and gave her a quick hug before she crossed the threshold.

"Oh, and don't call her a witch-- she hates that, and usually reacts badly to it. Good luck, blueberry. Remember to trust the training," said Gan

He must really be worried--he only calls me that when it's serious. As she turned to face the townhouse, the street faded behind her and was replaced by grass and dirt. Trees now surrounded the property. The townhouse was no longer on 26th Street. She looked around and saw that she was in a thick forest. She knew this place from her childhood. She came here as a little

26

girl, with her mother, a lifetime ago. A cold fist gripped her gut. She was in the park.

"Hello, Hunter."

Sepia turned to face the woman behind her. The woman she could only guess was Calisto stood next to the largest polar bear she had ever seen. Calisto was dressed in casual hiking clothes. Wearing dark jeans, hiking boots and a light sweater with her long brown hair pulled into a loose ponytail. She looked like a woman that enjoyed the outdoors-- it all fit, except the bear. The bear sitting on its haunches towered past Calisto's head. *I don't think I have enough ammo for that.* She reached for her guns and realized her holsters were empty. *The hug-- that sneaky bastard.* Only her sword remained, in its sheath.

"I don't usually get visitors," said Calisto as she turned to walk away from Sepia. The bear remained motionless, the light rippling over its silver coat. She could see the intelligence in its eyes. Calisto stood behind the bear now, stroking its hind quarters as she faced Sepia.

"Kill her," said Calisto.

The bear growled as it charged forward. Sepia rolled to the side, dodging the charge. *What I wouldn't do for some pepper spray right now.* The bear turned and stood on its hind quarters and reared toward her. Sepia backed away, trying to put a tree between them. The bear circled around and swiped. Sepia ducked the swipe and moved to the other side.

"Call off your pet. I only need to ask you some questions." She didn't want to kill this bear.

"You come to my home and demand answers? I see you are armed. Here is a question for you: Do you want to live?" said Calisto.

27

Sepia backpedaled as the bear jumped around the tree, forcing her to break away. *That is too damn smart for a bear.*

"Yes, I do."

Sepia was scared now. This fear was a familiar friend. It was that feeling in her gut that felt like the bottom had dropped out. The bear circled around her, its eyes starting to glow a dull green. *This is no bear.*

"Then I suggest you use your weapon," said Calisto.

The bear charged, its eyes a bright yellow now. Sepia knew she couldn't outrun it.

She drew her sword, its energy coursing through her. The blade turned black as she held it. The characters inscribed on the blade flashed red for a few seconds and then faded under the inky black covering.

The bear lunged and she managed to stop the claws from removing her arm by a fraction of a second. Breaking the parry she knelt on one knee and swiped in an arc across the floor. She cut deep into the bear's leg. It roared in pain, slamming a paw into her and sending her sprawling across the grass. She was certain her arm was broken where the bear connected. Her ink flushed with heat as it dealt with the injury, the pain threatening to rob her of consciousness. She looked around and realized her sword was lodged in the bear's leg. The bear reached down and pulled the sword from its leg, throwing it to one side. The bear then fixed its eyes on her, a growl in its throat as it drew closer.

"Enough. I have seen enough," said Calisto.

The bear stopped advancing and limped to Calisto's side. She placed a hand on its injury, healing it. She whispered something in its ear and it retreated to a deeper part of forest, leaving Calisto and Sepia alone.

"You are ill-equipped for this role, hunter."

Calisto walked over to where Sepia's sword, Perdition, rested, with a patch of dead grass surrounding it. It was still humming faintly. Calisto bent down and grabbed the hilt.

"No, don't!" Sepia yelled as she extended her arm.

The inky covering receded and the sword looked like an ordinary blade. Calisto held it up and examined it, reading the characters. She swiped the air a few times and lunged.

"This is a hard blade to forget. It has perfect balance. This is a blade of the twenty-one. This is Emiko's, your mother's blade."

Sepia nodded. Calisto swung it a few more times performing an intricate cross swipe with a double lunge. Sepia could see she was exceptionally skilled. She handed it back to Sepia, hilt-first.

"How are you…how are you even holding it?" Sepia asked, taken aback.

"Like I said, it is a fine ancient blade, but I am older than it. Its defenses can't harm me, though I can't use it like a hunter can. I can see it feels you are worthy to wield it, and yet you hesitate. Why?"

"The sword is evil, that's why," said Sepia.

Calisto laughed a throaty laugh that filled the park.

"The weapon is neither evil nor good. Its expression all depends on the wielder," said Calisto.

"Didn't you see it? Every time I draw it, it goes dark."

"That is not the blade. *You* are the cause of that, hunter. It is only a reflection of you."

"What?" *Can that be true? Can the darkness be coming from me?*

Calisto turned her head, distracted, as if she were listening to a far off voice.

"We don't have much time, so ask your questions," said Calisto.

"Last night a Nightmare was in my sector. A T6, if that means anything to you."

Calisto gave her a blank stare.

"I want to know how it got there. Aren't there wards around the park? How did it get past them?"

"Ah, the wards. Most of the wards in this city are quite old. Usually they grow weaker with age, but not those."

"What's different about them?"

Sepia can see that the grass is reverting to concrete. As she looked around, the forest was slowly fading away.

"The wards around the park draw their energy from each new day. Each morning those wards are infused with new power, so they never lose their charge," Calisto explains.

"Who could do such a thing, then? Who could get past them?"

"The knowledge to do so is beyond me," said Calisto.

"Can a Nightmare get through a ward on its own?"

"These creatures you call Nightmares cannot destroy wards like these. It would require a power several orders of magnitude beyond them. Even I would have difficulty."

"What kind of power?"

Calisto pointed at Sepia's sword.

"It would need an ancient power and a conduit, a person who could wield the power. A power, like the one contained in your sword."

Sepia noticed that the townhouse was once again on 26ᵗʰ Street. When she looked around she saw Gan across the street. As she crossed over the threshold Calisto held her arm.

"A word of caution, hunter. You must surrender to the power contained within your weapon. Harness it, embrace it, before it destroys you or worse."

What can be worse than destruction? As she turned to Calisto she realized the townhouse was fading again. She heard her voice on the wind.

"Tell Gan to come and visit me when he is free." Calisto's laughter echoed in her mind.

Gan handed her the guns when she crossed the street.

"That was sneaky, even for you," said Sepia as she holstered her guns.

"Better I take them than Calisto. At least now you can get them back, with her you would have lost them and earned a few scars in the process."

They walked for a few minutes in silence, stopping at the corner of 23ʳᵈ and Lexington.

"At least you survived. Not every hunter makes it out of her house intact."

"It felt familiar somehow. That place, I think I've been there before."

"Wouldn't surprise me. You spent a lot of time there as a child. Calisto, she helped train your mother," says Gan.

"She did what?"

Gan turned to walk away, stopping after a few steps.

"I have another meeting to get to. You have a few hours before your tour, so go get some shuteye. I suggest you go on patrol and find out how a T6 wound up in your neighborhood. That's my advice, for all it's worth."

She knew better than to press him, but she was worried about this meeting of his. *How does he even know Calisto? It certainly looks like she knew him.*

"Oh, Calisto had a message for you. She said to go visit her when you were free. You two have a thing?"

Gan laughed as he walked away.

"Visit her? Not in this lifetime. You be careful tonight, blueberry," said Gan.

SEVEN

SEPIA CAUGHT THE 6 TRAIN downtown to Canal and walked along Canal Street to her apartment on West Street.

Every hunter lived in their sector. It made it easier for them to patrol. She had a few hours before nightfall and sleep sounded like a great idea. Entry into her building was secure. It required a keypad combination and a handprint. Many of the newer developments were using this heightened level of security. When the elevator arrived on her floor she knew something was off. Seeing the door to her apartment ajar, she drew her guns and nudged the door wider with them. Her apartment was trashed.

"What the hell?"

She walked in and realized the break in was systematic. Someone was looking for something. There went her few hours of sleep. *Sun is setting anyway. May as well get a head start on tonight's patrol,* she thought as she pulled out her phone and speed dialed Cade.

"Blue. Feeling better?" He sounded strange, his voice thick.

"Not much, my apartment got trashed and I haven't gotten any sleep. Where are you? Let's head in early tonight. I think I want to walk the lower perimeter of the park and see if there's a breach."

"I was kind of hoping you could tell me, um where I am. I don't have a clue," said Cade.

Another voice came on the phone.

"Hello, hunter. You want him alive? Bring the sword to his location. Oh, and I would hurry if I were you."

Cade began to scream as her stomach tightened into a knot. The phone went dead.

She pressed another speed dial as she headed out the apartment, taking the stairs two at a time.

"Gan, they got Cade."

"It's a trap. Do not go to his location."

"What are you saying? I should leave him to die?"

"I'm saying you shouldn't go, at least not alone. Where are you?"

"I'm at the apartment. If you're coming, you have five minutes or I'm getting Cade without you," she said as she hung up.

Gan looked at his phone. *God she is stubborn, just like her mother.* He turned his motorcycle around and headed to Sepia's apartment. From his location he could make it there in three minutes.

Sepia stood perfectly still calming her breathing. Geolocation depended on the hunter being able to function in spite of distraction. She quieted her mind and tried to pick up Cade's vibration with no success. A few minutes passed and then a motorcycle raced up the street, distracting her.

"Did you find him?" Gan said as he took off his helmet.

"I was in the middle of that."

She closed her eyes again and extended herself. This time she felt Cade's presence. It was a faint sensation and getting fainter.

She jumped on the back of the motorcycle.

"He's north, towards the park," she said.

"Did you call Home yet?"

"Shit, it totally slipped my mind."

"You know the Order, Blue. No matter what, you follow protocol, especially in the field."

She sighed. "I know. Hunters follow procedure, no matter what. The training saves lives."

"I'll take care of it. Let's go get your partner," Gan said as they pulled off with a roar.

They sped up Sixth Avenue. The queasy feeling in his stomach reminded him why he hated being this close to the park.

They were approaching the lower end of the park when Sepia tapped his helmet.

"Whose sector is this?" Sepia asked as she looked around. She could see the wards glowing faintly at the edge of the park.

A block away Gan turned off the motorcycle. He wanted to make sure they had a way to get out of there fast.

"We walk from here; I'm not risking the bike. We're in Lisa's and Xavier's sector. Turn off your phone. You know what the park can do."

"I know, I know, no electronics. Are they any good? Lisa and Xavier?" Sepia said as she tried to pinpoint Cade's location.

"Two of the best, or else they wouldn't be so close to the park."

"How did a Nightmare get past them if they are so good?"

"Why don't you ask them yourself?" Gan pointed with his chin.

"What? What do you mean?"

A figure stepped out of the shadows directly in front of them, seeming to materialize from air. He was a wiry man of dark complexion with fire in his eyes.

"Gan, it has been too long. How are you, you old dog?"

It was Xavier.

Does Gan know everyone? Who is he?

"It has been too long, X. Where's Lisa?"

"She's headed to the park. Some commotion up there. I was just about to follow her. Had some low level trouble to take care of a few blocks down."

"She's going in there alone?" said Gan as he started heading into the park.

Xavier read Gan's face and took off at a dead run toward the park, stopping at the edge.

"What is that? It's like we're above a train station, a low rumbling," said Sepia.

"It's the park. It gives off a constant low frequency EMP wave," said Gan.

"It's never felt that strong."

"Do you think she went in?" Xavier peered into the darkness.

"Only one way to find out," said Gan

He turned to face Sepia, as she checked her guns and holstered them.

"I would tell you to wait here, but I know better. Be careful, once you cross this threshold, all bets are off. No cavalry is coming to save our asses. We are on our own."

"He is in there. I can feel him. He's still alive, Gan."

"Who's in there? Is someone else in there?" asked Xavier

"Her gunman was taken, but I think it's a trap for her, and Lisa walked right into it."

"Shit. Why do they want you?"

Anger shone in Xavier's eyes as drew his handguns and strapped his rifle to his back.

"Xavier, does Lisa have a named blade?" asked Sepia.

Xavier's eyes narrowed.

"I can't tell you. Don't you know that? Who is this rookie?"

"That's enough of an answer. She must be a class one."

"Easy, X, Lisa is a class one with a named blade, she can handle most things in there," said Gan.

"She is *the* class one. Yeah, her blade is named. It's one bastard of a blade. How do you think we can be so close to the park and still be alive?"

They stepped over the threshold and into the park. Sepia felt it thrum her entire body like a tuning fork.

"We need to find her fast. Whatever they were going to do with me…"

Sepia let the words hang in the air after seeing Xavier's expression. *These two are more than just hunter and gunman. He really cares for her. I wonder how long they have been out here.*

"You locate Cade, we will find Lisa," said Gan.

Sepia extended herself again and found Cade. He was close now.

"That way," she said and pointed.

She took off at a jog with Gan and Xavier right behind her. They heard the clashing of blades first before they saw anyone.

"That's her. I'd recognize that sound anywhere," said Xavier.

"Took you long enough, X" said Lisa. "What? You stop for dinner?"

Her left side was covered in blood. She had numerous cuts and scratches on her arms, some of them deep and bleeding freely. The Nightmare Lisa was fighting was unlike any Sepia had encountered.

Lisa parried a thrust and dodged a slash aimed at her midsection. She was trying to lure the Nightmare away from Cade, with little success. The Nightmare held a short sword designed for close-quarter fighting. Sepia could see it was skilled, but Lisa was holding her own against it.

"Where do you want me?" said Xavier. He started to unstrap his rifle.

"No, X, grab the gunman when you can and get as far from here as possible," said Lisa.

"What? Hell no. I am not leaving you in here alone. Not happening."

He pulled out two hunting knives and drew closer to the Nightmare.

"You are one stubborn son of a bitch," said Lisa.

"That's why you love me," said Xavier.

Xavier turned to Gan and smiled. It was full of ferocity and something else: resignation.

"I'm going to pull that fucker away from your gunman. When I do, you grab him and haul ass. Don't wait for us, don't even look back."

"Xavier, don't do this. We can all get out of here," said Sepia.

"Who said we aren't? My lady and I have plans later tonight and they don't involve dying," said Xavier.

Xavier placed his rifle on the floor and slid closer to the Nightmare.

"Remember what I said. You grab your man and run. Run like every Nightmare in here is on your ass, because they probably will be."

Xavier jumped into the fray and managed to move the Nightmare away from Cade. Lisa took a step back and circled around, creating more space between them and the bound gunman.

Sepia made a move to draw her sword but Gan stopped her.

"Don't, not in here. That will bring us more than we can handle, which is not much at the moment."

Sepia looked questioningly at Gan.

"I'll explain later. Go get Cade."

They ran over to Cade. He fell to the ground as they cut his bonds. His shirt was soaked in blood and Sepia couldn't feel a pulse.

Don't be dead, don't be dead, don't be dead, goddammit, Sepia thought as they carried him away from the fighting.

"He's alive but barely. Let's get you two out of here," said Gan.

They made their way to the edge of the park and Gan turned to go back.

"Where are you going?"

"I'm not going to let those two throw their lives away playing hero. Get Cade to the main infirmary. Don't tell anyone where this happened, not yet. Wait until I get there. Lie if you have to." He handed her the keys to the bike and headed back in to the park.

Sepia carried Cade back to the motorcycle and strapped him in. She started the engine and it roared to life. Cade stirred on her back and she placed another strap around the both of them, keeping him upright.

"Stay with me, Cade. Stay with me," she said.

She looked back to see Gan running back into the park. For a moment it looked as if his hands were glowing with the same energy as the wards.

EIGHT

G AN CAME BACK INTO the park and saw them. A few moments more and both hunter and gunman would fall. The Nightmare was growing stronger, its blows faster and more precise. Life and death were measured in these moments. He ran toward them.

Lisa dodged a slash that would have removed a leg, only to be hit by a barrage of black globules. Her right side began to sizzle as she threw off her jacket. Some of the black globules had penetrated her leather and burned her skin.

"Lisa!" yelled Xavier. He saw the black ooze hit her squarely in the side.

"I'm okay. It didn't get in too deep," she lied as she switched hands. Her sword arm was useless, the numbness making it dead weight.

Xavier lunged with both knives. The Nightmare parried both strikes, sending Xavier's arms to the sides and creating an opening and kicking him in the chest, sending him sprawling. Xavier managed to look up in time to see Gan approaching the Nightmare.

I'm getting too old for this, Gan thought as the Nightmare approached his new target. Gan took a fighting stance as Xavier ran over to where Lisa leaned against a tree.

"You two should get out of here," said Gan. "This is going to get ugly fast."

"No way, old man," said Xavier. You stay, we stay."

Gan shook his head at their stubbornness. *I would have stayed too, if only to see if the old man had anything left besides, those two couldn't leave even if they wanted to.*

"It's your funeral," Gan said.

The Nightmare's face betrayed no emotion as it squared against Gan. It lunged as Gan shifted his weight to one side allowing the blade to pass beside him. The Nightmare sliced across, but Gan was already under the blade and moving in. *Where the hell is she?* Gan slammed a palm into the inner thigh of the Nightmare forcing it back. The muscles of the Nightmare's leg imploded, leaving a palm sized depression. Staggering back a few steps, the Nightmare hissed in pain as its leg regenerated. The Nightmare swiped its blade down in a diagonal arc and then up trying to catch Gan off balance as he evaded the strikes. Gan waited for the last strike to reach its apex and struck the sword arm, impacting the triceps. Switching hands the Nightmare assumed a defensive stance as he circled Gan. *This is like spitting in the wind, it regenerates faster than I can do damage,* thought Gan.

Xavier and Lisa watched from the side. Xavier kept his knives drawn in case they had more visitors.

"That stance, wait, he's fighting like a--" said Xavier.

"He's fighting like a hunter," said Lisa as she collapsed to one knee. The poison was making its way through her body. Paralysis would set in first and respiratory arrest soon after.

"Hang in there, girl," said Xavier. "We need to get you the hell out of here. The old man was right," said Xavier under his breath.

"Don't think I'll be going anywhere for a while. I can't feel my right leg."

"Shit," said Xavier.

He moved fast and cut open her pants leg and saw the network of small black lines that looked like an intricate spider web slowly spreading down her leg.

"That thing is a widow, Gan. Lisa's been hit, and we are running out of time," said Xavier as he took one of the blades and made a cut below the progressing lines, drawing out the blood that was being infected. Black liquid seeped from the wound.

"I'm working on it, X, but this thing is not cooperating," said Gan.

Gan circled around the Nightmare. Widows were bad news; this one was at least a T5. *No problem, all I have to do is not get hit. Should be a walk in the park.* The Nightmare moved in, its arm regenerated. Kicking low, it attempted to shatter Gan's knee. Gan saw it for the feint it was and rather than stepping back into sword range, stepped forward and jammed the kick. Blocking the sword arm and driving a palm into the Nightmare's chest, he forced it down. *I can't do this for much longer. Getting tired.* The Nightmare pushed up, shoving a shoulder into Gan. It whirled around, blade-first, forcing Gan back out of its deadly circle.

"How can he fight that thing with no weapon?" said Xavier.

"His hands, look at his hands -he's using the stone palm. I wouldn't be surprised if he was inked as well," said Lisa.

"I thought only hunters could use that technique?" said Xavier.

Gan slid into the Nightmare, jumping up at the last second and attacked with both hands in what looked like a shove. The Nightmare brought up its sword in time to block one of Gan's hands. The blade shattered on impact. His other hand thrown off by the deflection crashed into the Nightmare's shoulder, pushing it back and out of range.

Lisa's breathing was becoming labored and her brow was covered in sweat. Xavier looked at Gan's hands and realized for the first time that they were glowing. The glow was getting dimmer as Gan continued fighting.

"That can't be good," whispered Xavier.

The Nightmare tossed away the useless blade and raised its hand. The hand was enveloped with a dark energy extending up the forearm.

"Time to die," said the Nightmare as it smiled at Gan.

Gan knew it was over. He was too close. It would be like dodging a shotgun blast at point blank range. He braced for the impact when an arrow shaft appeared in the Nightmare's hand followed by several more in its body. The arrows were crystalline shafts with diamond-tipped arrowheads. The Nightmare began to howl in pain. Gan raced in, grabbed the haft of one of the arrows and pulled it free. The Nightmare roared at him. Arrow in hand, he plunged it into the Nightmare's eye. It fell to the ground, clawing at its face as it disintegrated.

"You cut that one a little close, don't you think?" Gan said into the park. He was breathing hard and his hands were steaming in the night.

"I was busy elsewhere. It would seem this is a battle fought on several fronts," a female voice answered from the night.

It was Calisto. In her hand she held a power crossbow. Across her back rested a quiver of arrows with diamond-tip arrowheads, each arrow a small fortune. Calisto retrieved her arrows from the dust that was the Nightmare. Dressed in black camouflage, she looked like a living shadow. Knives adorned both her thighs, each blade gleaming in the night.

"No time for talk, since that was just a distraction. More will be coming. She was of no use to them," she said as she pointed to Lisa with her chin. "I can hold them for a short time, but they will come," said Calisto.

Gan shook his hands to get the feeling back in them, pins and needles shooting up his arms.

"You used the palms," said Calisto as she looked down at Gan's hands. "You know the risks."

"Didn't have a choice, it was either that or they died," he said as he looked at Lisa and Xavier.

There was a crash in the distance.

"That sounds angry," said Gan.

It sounded like several trees being uprooted and thrown at once. Xavier lifted Lisa up and helped her limp her way out of the park.

"Who the hell is that?" Xavier said as he glanced at Calisto.

"I don't know. All I know is that she saved all our asses, even Gan's," mumbled Lisa clearly in pain.

"Go. Ursa and I will keep them busy here. You must not let them get to Sepia," said Calisto.

A large silver bear padded over to where she stood eyeing Gan warily. Gan bowed his head to the bear. The bear sat on its haunches and stared at Gan before giving a slight nod. They were at the edge of the park now and the noise was getting closer. It sounded like the earth was being ripped apart.

"Why Sepia? What is so special about her?"

Gan said as he placed an arm under Lisa to speed her along.

"That is what you need to find out. These breaches are not an accident. They are getting more frequent and are leading up to something. Find out why her blade goes dark when she wields it," said Calisto.

The noise was threatening to deafen them. Calisto turned to face it. With a gesture, a wall of earth and stone rose before her, slowing the sound.

"Now go," she said.

Calisto started walking toward the wall she erected. She faded into the night trailed by Ursa. The bear moved without making a sound as it bounded after her.

"You need to get her to the infirmary," said Gan.

"The one in our sector is down. A Nightmare trashed it two nights ago. We have to go to the one over in sector nine. I can get us there in fifteen," said Xavier.

Gan helped Lisa into their vehicle. It was a sporty two-seater, built for speed.

"I would drop you somewhere, but…" said Xavier.

"No need. Go get her some help. I'll make my way back."

"Thanks, old man," said Xavier.

"Get moving," said Gan as he slammed the top of the vehicle. Xavier took off, tires screeching as he headed down Sixth Avenue the wrong way and made a turn to the sector infirmary several blocks away.

"I have a few stops to make in either case," Gan said as he took off at a run.

NINE

SEPIA HATED MOTORCYCLES. *Moving coffins is what they are.* Behind her, Cade grunted. *The only benefit these things have is that they could move fast when needed. Why would Gan want me to take him to the main infirmary, when each sector has one and I'm going to have to go through several sectors on my way there?*

Cade shifted again and her heart lurched.

"Don't die on me, Cade. You hear me?" she yelled over the roar of the bike's engine.

The high pitched whine of the engine was the only response she received. Getting to 82nd and Fifth took twelve minutes. She didn't stop for red lights or traffic, using sidewalks when she could. She drove the bike right into the waiting room where medical personnel removed Cade from the bike and placed him on a gurney.

"We got him, Miss. Blue. Can you please take the bike outside?" one of the nurses said.

"Huh, what? Oh, I'm sorry, yeah. I'll do that."

Her eyes followed Cade as they wheeled him away. She still held his bloody shirt in her hands. Tucking the shirt into her jacket she grabbed the bike and began rolling it to the garage. She found a parking space near the entrance.

"That was your fault, you know."

Sepia turned to face the woman speaking. She was a tall figure, all legs in dark red leathers, leaning against one of the columns. Her piercing blue eyes were bloodshot. Cigarette smoke floated lazily from her hand. She gazed at Sepia with a mixture of hatred and pity. The hat she wore kept most of her face in shadow, but Sepia could tell what she was--a hunter.

"Excuse me, do I know you?" Sepia said, the edge in her voice a clear warning. *I don't have time for pissing contests tonight.*

"I lost my gunman tonight, hunter. He was a good friend."

"Listen, I'm sorry for your loss, but I don't know you."

The hunter pointed a finger at Sepia as she spoke.

"Did you hear me? I lost my gunman and yours is in there fighting for his life because of you. You are a sorry excuse for a hunter. How did a class two nobody get a named blade anyway? Think I would take my chances with the Nightmares than have you watch my back," she said and then spat on the floor. Sepia clenched a fist. *I don't have time for this shit,* she thought.

The figure stepped off the column and drew close to Sepia. Sepia put a hand on her holster. The woman laughed, it was full of grief.

"I wish you would try. You think because your mother was some famous hunter, that you get a free pass? That there won't be consequences? I had to earn my class. It wasn't given to me because of Mommy."

"Fuck off." Sepia turned and started to walk away.

"Something asked for you tonight, Sepia Blue."

46

Sepia stopped midstride and turned to face the hunter.

"Look, I don't know you and frankly I don't want to know-" said Sepia.

The hunter drew close to Sepia.

"My name is Jen. My enemies know me as Red Jen and you? Well you'd better watch your back."

The woman crushed the cigarette in the wall, turned and walked off as a nurse was coming to get Sepia.

"Doctor Clark would like to see you, Miss. Blue," said the nurse.

"What a bitch," said Sepia. The nurse turned and looked at the figure walking away.

"Oh, that's Jen Rodriguez. They call her Red Jen. She always wears red leathers when she is out on patrol. Dangerous Hunter I hear."

"What is her problem?"

"Rough night on patrol, lost her gunman and she almost died too. Her gunman was killed while she was covering another hunter's sector tonight."

"Which sector was she covering?"

The nurse looked down at her clipboard and turned a few pages over.

"It says here she was covering sector thirteen."

Oh shit, my sector, thought Sepia.

The nurse entered the infirmary and pointed to the door where the doctor waited for her. As she made her way to the door the nurse grabbed her by the hand and placed a small piece of paper in her palm. It was done so fast she almost didn't notice. Sepia turned back to see if she could see the hunter, but Jen was gone.

She was about to open her hand when the nurse signaled her not to.

"The doctor is waiting for you, Miss. Blue," the nurse said as she clasped her hand around Sepia's.

"Not here," she whispered. "You have eyes on you."

She put her hand on the small of Sepia's back and guided her to the doctor's office.

The doctor turned as Sepia entered his office. He was a balding older man, who was once physically fit, but was seeing a bit of bulge in his later years. He adjusted his bifocals as Sepia entered his office.

"Hello, I'm Doctor Clark. You can call me Arthur. I am the chief of the floor tonight. I need to know how your partner," he paused to type a few keys on his computer. " a Mr. Kincade, received his injuries?"

"Cade. He hates Kincade. He got his injuries during our patrol," she lied.

"Miss. Blue, may I call you Sepia?" She nodded.

"I am a doctor who treats hunters. That means I have seen it all. Lying to me is not going to help your gunman."

"We were on patrol when we were ambushed. I managed to get him away, but not before he was hurt." *Why am I lying to this man? Gan, I hope you're right.*

"I see. It seems that the injuries he sustained indicate he was restrained for a prolonged period of time. Do you have any idea how long?"

"No, I don't."

Doctor Clark tapped away at his keyboard.

"You understand that withholding information is only going to make my job harder, right? I already lost one gunman tonight. I don't want to make it two. Can you tell me anything?"

The doctor looked weary. His eyes were bloodshot and only reminded Sepia that she needed sleep. The exhaustion suddenly caught up with her and she sagged in her chair. She had no reason to distrust him.

"He, we, were in the park. A Nightmare had him. It was a setup, to trap me."

The doctor remained calm as he made some notes, and continued typing on his keyboard.

"That would explain some of the lacerations. Do you know how long he was held? Try to think, Sepia. Was it two hours, three?"

"I don't know, maybe three–four hours? I got the call in the early evening and Gan told me he left the hospital early."

"Who is Gan?" said the Doctor.

"How is that relevant to treating Cade?"

"I have to place all present parties during the time of the injury."

"Are you going to put down the Nightmare that did this to him, too? Should I get you its info?" She was getting angrier by the second.

"This is just a formality, Sepia. I need to file an incident report, especially if this occurred in the park. You do know the park is off-limits to hunters?"

She glared daggers at him, regretting telling him anything. *Typical bureaucrat, everything is red tape and procedure,* she thought.

He tapped his keyboard some more and adjusted his bifocals as he looked up at Sepia. The note in her hand felt heavy. *What does the nurse want?*

"Can you tell me what you were doing in the park?"

"No, I can't, and I don't see how this is helping Cade."

"I can assure you Mr. Kincade will get the best treatment possible. Excuse me while I make some calls."

As he stood up, he put a hand on her shoulder, a gesture of comfort. She knew then she had made a mistake telling him.

"Thank you, Sepia, if you would just wait here, I'll be back shortly."

"Sure, thank you, Doctor Clark."

"Arthur, please call me Arthur."

"Where is the bathroom around here?" Sepia said as she stood.

"Two doors down on your right, and I'll be right back."

Everything was telling her something was off. *What is with the interrogation?* She entered the bathroom and found an empty stall. Opening the small piece of paper, she saw the scrawled handwriting. There were only four words. Four words that gut-punched her.

Cade not here--RUN.

She flushed the paper and stepped out of the bathroom. *Why would they take Cade and where?* She never liked the smell of hospitals. They smelled of death and despair. She always found them sterile and cold. She looked at the exit and saw hospital security stationed there. As she made her way to the garage, she heard the footfalls behind her.

"Miss. Blue, a moment please."

It was another security guard.

She blasted through the door and ran to the bike. Leaning against it was a man dressed in a dark suit, his bronze skin contrasting against his white shirt. He had a gun in his hand.

"Hello, Blue, long time," said the suit. He had a slight accent; each word was a crisp breath. *That voice, can it be, Ronin? It can't be.* Her hand flew to her holster. His face was different, but she could never forget that voice.

"We can do this the easy way or the hard way, your choice," said the suit.

Sepia drew her pistol and almost got the shot off. She was stopped as she raised her arm. Every muscle in her body contracted as fifty thousand volts slammed her to the ground. The pain that followed overwhelmed her defenses and the world grew dark.

"The hard way, then," said the suit.

T E N

JONATHAN MARKS SAT BEHIND the large table and looked at the seated figure before him. They were in one of the interrogation sites, an empty cell, two doors, two chairs and a table. He waited patiently until Sepia regained consciousness. He sat back and steepled his fingers as she came to.

"Hello, Sepia. Welcome back," said Marks.

Her weapons were gone and she was chained to the chair, which was bolted to the ground. She pulled against them anyway, testing their limits.

"That chain was made with hunters in mind, but if you must, please, feel free."

She knew it was pointless. So she sat motionless.

"You tazed me?"

"It was a necessary precaution. You drew on me," said Marks.

Aside from an intense soreness that was quickly dissipating thanks to her ink, she felt almost normal.

"Where's Cade?" She was feeling stronger by the moment.

"I'm sure he's safe and being treated for his injuries. Those were some nasty injuries by the way," said Marks. "Do you know who I am?"

"Should I know you? You look like another suit to me," said Sepia. "Speaking of which, where is this? We aren't Home."

She could tell from the cell that she was in one of the offsite facilities. One of the places where the Order made people disappear.

"My name is Jonathan Marks and I am second to the Overseer for Manhattan South."

"Oh, you work for the head suit." *God, hate these types, in an office all day never setting foot in the field, too good to get their hands dirty.*

"I am the head suit, Miss. Blue. The Overseer is just what you would call a figurehead position. I don't think you understand the gravity of your situation, Miss. Blue," said Marks.

"Educate me." *That voice. He sounds just like Ronin, but that's impossible. I killed Ronin.*

"You violated a standing order against entering a restricted area. I have one gunman dead and your gunman was critically injured in some strange attempt to capture you."

"I had nothing to do with that," said Sepia.

"Regardless, you were the catalyst."

"You know as much as I do, probably more," said Sepia.

"Oh, on that we can agree," said Marks.

Marks stood from the table and faced the wall sized mirror, his hands behind his back. Sepia followed the motion, knowing that behind that mirror others were watching. He turned to face her again.

"You know what I find even more disturbing? I am seeing high threat level creatures breaching a ward that is supposed to be unbreachable, and they are asking for you by name, Miss. Blue."

"How the hell am I supposed to know anything about that?"

"I hear you are having trouble with your sword," said Marks matter-of- factly.

"What? What the hell?" He caught her off-guard.

"Well, how does a hunter with your obvious pedigree have a problem with a named blade?"

Marks leaned against the mirror and crossed his arms, never taking his eyes off of her.

"I, I don't know, I'm just not focusing enough. I'm still working through it," said Sepia, flustered.

"Do you realize a man died while handling your blade? Completely absorbed him, turned to dust I believe the reports say."

"I'm going to guess he tried removing it from its scabbard. Don't you suits know anything? You never touch a hunter's blade," said Sepia, the anger returning.

"Tell me, Miss. Blue, how do you explain the blackouts? Can you explain the obvious exponential increase in strength, and the fact that you took a Threat level 6 Nightmare on your own?"

"I can't."

"I have a theory. Would you like to hear it?"

Sepia lifted her arms, raising the chains around her wrists. The heavy links rattled and fell to the floor, pulling her arms down.

"Doesn't look like I'm going anywhere," said Sepia.

"Well, before I share it, I'd like to discuss your eyes."

"My eyes? Really?" said Sepia.

Marks walked over to the table and sat down, looking at Sepia. He placed both hands on the table and leaned forward.

"There is one other creature we know of that has eyes like yours," said Marks.

He placed special emphasis on the word 'creature'. It had the desired effect.

"It's a specific type of Nightmare," he said, lowering his voice.

Sepia lunged at him, but the chains held her in place. Marks didn't register her movement.

"Fuck you," she said.

"Like I was saying, this type of Nightmare is somewhat rare and was only documented once, thirty years ago. After killing twenty veteran hunters, two of which had named blades, it was able to escape back into the park."

"Your point?" said Sepia.

"Do you recall your father, Sepia?" The question threw her. *What the fuck?* were the only words she could form.

54

"My father was killed when I was born. If you're with the Overseer, you know this. What the hell are you trying to say?"

"Your eyes, Miss. Blue, they only point to one logical conclusion. You are the child of a Nightmare and a human," said Marks.

He sat back as Sepia looked at him in shock.

"Sir," a voice came over the intercom. "We have a perimeter breach. One vehicle carrying one passenger, armed."

The building was rocked by an explosion. Sepia sat still, dumbfounded. *Could it be true? Could her father be a Nightmare?*

Marks turned to the mirror.

"Find out what that was. I have no intention of losing our guest here." He pointed at Sepia.

Smoke filled the corridor and crept in under the door. The door behind Sepia began to bulge in. Marks opened the other door and allowed the pressure to regulate. The door settled into the frame and then exploded inwards. Marks avoided the brunt of the blast and pulled out his gun.

The door missed Sepia and bounced into the mirrored wall, shattering it. Sepia could see the monitors inside and the group of Unholy that were coming for her. Marks shot the first figure that entered the room. Several more of the Unholy were making their way down the corridor to Sepia's location.

"It would seem this is a battle for another day, Miss. Blue. Think about what I told you. Do us all a favor and kill yourself now while you still can. It looks like your father's side of the family has come to get you." He spat out the last sentence with a hatred that was palpable.

He opened the other door and ran out of the room, shooting as he ran. Sepia took stock of her situation. *I am not going to die here.* She had maybe ten seconds before they found her. She pulled on the chains until they cut into her skin, drawing blood. Pulling with all her strength, she strained until she saw spots dancing in her eyes. The bolts groaned and snapped as she ripped the chains out of the floor. The hanging chains mocked her, mute reminders that she was more than a hunter. Another explosion rocked the building, threatening to collapse the structure.

Sepia ran down a corridor. *Where am I? This is definitely an offsite but where?* She saw that the building was an old industrial facility, once used as a stapler factory judging from the worn signs. She carefully made her way around the hallways. The smoke and noise were disorienting. Unholy ran in the corridors. She felt unarmed until she looked down at her wrists. She wrapped the chains once around each hand. It left her with a three foot length of chain hanging from each one. *It's not a sword but it will do.* She caught one of the minions by the neck and dragged him to the ground. *Where is the Nightmare?* The minions were pretty mindless and would need the direction of a Nightmare to coordinate their movements. These were too organized to be here alone. A Nightmare had to be in the building.

"Sepia!" she heard someone yell behind her.

"Gan?" She must be imagining things. Why would Gan be here? How did he find her?

Looking through the haze of smoke she saw a figure that could only be her old trainer.

"Who else? Get your ass over here, before we're overrun. These guys have a real hard-on for you," said Gan.

She could just make out Gan in the smoke-filled corridor. He threw her a gun. She used both hands to catch it because of the chains. Turning, she shot two of the Unholy that came down the corridor.

"What the hell are those? Accessories?" Gan said looking at the chains.

She held up the other chain to show him the cuffs.

"Hunter restraints, the latest in fashion," said Sepia.

"We'll deal with that later. Let's get out of here, go!"

They ran out the door into a large asphalt lot. An SUV with tinted windows was sitting there with the doors open and the engine running. Gan took off at a run.

"That's our ride, move it blueberry!"

She ran beside him and they reached the vehicle and jumped in. Gan jumped in the driver's side and took off. Another explosion collapsed the roof of the building, compromising its integrity. The building fell in on itself belching fire and smoke everywhere.

"Cade?" Sepia whispered as she looked at the inferno behind her.

"He wasn't in there with you. We intercepted him before they moved him out of the Main Infirmary."

"That's why you wanted me to go to the Main. Where are we?"

"Queens. Long Island City to be precise," said Gan.

"Are we heading back in?"

She looked back at the burnt out husk that was the factory. The fire would burn for hours, it seemed.

Gan nodded as he checked his mirrors. He made sure they weren't being followed before he headed to the 59th Street Bridge. No one called it the Koch Bridge.

"What the hell are the Unholy doing way out here?" said Sepia.

"I was just about to ask you the same thing," said Gan.

"Who was leading this op, Sepia?"

"It was a suit, went by the name of Marks, Jonathan Marks."

"The Overseer's right hand?" *Why would he be out here dealing with a hunter?* "What did he say to you?"

Sepia looked out the window. She couldn't face him and tell him what Marks had told her.

"C'mon, Blue, you know you can tell me anything," said Gan as he swerved to avoid bridge traffic.

She decided to change the subject.

"How did you find me, Gan?"

He knew this was a delaying tactic. She had used it ever since she was a little girl. He lifted up his wrist and showed her a bracelet similar to the one she wore. Encrusted in it were small blue gems.

"Your bracelet. The gems are keyed to each other. I can find you anywhere within a ten-mile radius. I tracked you from the infirmary and followed your escort here," said Gan.

She looked at her bracelet.

"Can this screw with my geolocation?"

"Hmm, I didn't think of that, it's possible. In any case, I thought it strange that the Order would be heading out to Queens in the middle of the night unless something major was happening. You turned out to be the major something."

"I've only heard the stories about the off-sites. It's where they make people vanish. I didn't think they were real," she said.

Gan nodded.

"Too real for my taste," said Gan. "Want to tell me what he said, Blue?"

"He said my father--" her voice caught in her throat. "He said my father was some kind of rare Nightmare. He said that's the reason for these," she said pointing at her eyes. "He said it's why I blackout and I can't align with my sword."

The words came out fast and hurried. The tears started then and she wiped her face.

"Sepia, that's a lie," said Gan.

She turned to face him, angry. Her jaw was clenched along with her fists.

"Calm down, Blue, it's never been heard of before. In all the time I've been with the Order, there has never been a documented case of a child born from Nightmares. Those things are made, they don't have parents," said Gan.

She wanted to believe him, but it still nagged at her. Marks was too convincing.

 "I'm going to need to access the archives," she said.

"That's going to be tricky, since the Archives are secured under Home. Besides, what will that prove?"

"He said something about an incident thirty years ago, so maybe I can find out more about that Nightmare," said Sepia.

Gan knew which incident Marks was referring to. *Bryant Park. Maybe it's time she knew the truth.*

"I think it's a waste of time, but if you have to know, we'll send someone. You can't go," said Gan. "I don't know if Marks is acting alone or as an extension of your Overseer. Until then, Home is off-limits."

-"You can't go Home again," she said to herself and laughed, the nervous laughter borne of fear and stress.

"Blue, that was horrible. I stand by what I said though. I've never heard of a Nightmare child. I will get it checked out, though."

"It makes sense, Gan. Every other hunter I know with this much time on the job doesn't have a problem with their blades."

"You don't know all of the hunters, especially not the named blades. They have practiced and trained much harder than you, Sepia."

"What if he's right? What if I'm part Nightmare?"

"As unlikely as that is, it still wouldn't change who or what you are. You are a hunter."

"It would change everything."

She looked out of the window at the approaching skyline.

I know she is right, if it's true would I be able to protect her? They crossed the bridge and Gan turned left onto Second Avenue heading downtown.

"Let's go get Cade," said Gan.

ELEVEN

THEY WERE BACK IN Sepia's sector.

"If Nightmares are looking for you this is where they would look: your sector."

"So I'm bait now?" said Sepia.

"Yes, unless you know why they want you and a better way to attract them?" Gan offered. "Let's go over to Broadway and take the Westside Highway. That should expose you plenty."

Gan left the truck on Canal Street, the Order plates assuring it wouldn't get towed. They started walking. Sepia felt hyper alert expecting an attack at any moment. Gan took out her weapons from the back and handed them to her. She strapped her sword to her back, the weight a welcome comfort. Each gun rested in its holster.

"He sounded like Ronin," said Sepia.

"Who did?" Gan looked at her, concern etched in his face.

"Marks did. I swear, if I didn't look at his face, I would have thought Ronin was in front me."

"You took care of Ronin, remember?"

Gan didn't like where this was going.

"*Remember*? I put three bullets in his chest. How could I forget?"

"Ronin is long gone, you're just tired. When was the last time you slept?"

"Two, three days. I haven't had time."

Gan stopped walking and looked at her.

"What do you mean you haven't had time?"

"What with everything that's been happening, and Cade. Then I got tazed--does that count? I don't remember how long I was out," said Sepia.

"Getting yourself tazed doesn't count. Wait, who tazed you?"

"Marks did, and I almost shot him when I heard his voice," said Sepia.

"You are a piece of work, Blue." Gan was smiling in spite of himself.

"I was on edge. I had just spoken to Jen. She lost her gunman patrolling my sector."

"I heard. It was a rough night all around. That doesn't mean you shoot first and ask questions later," he said.

"It was a reflex, that's all," she said.

They stopped in front of an old tenement building.

"We're going in here?" said Sepia.

"This is where your partner is recovering," said Gan.

"You're kidding. This looks like a rat-infested dump," said Sepia.

"It's supposed to look like that. As a new class two you're not supposed to know about Grey sites. That's why I had you head to the main infirmary. I didn't think they would be waiting for you. This is called hiding in plain sight. Something you will have to learn to do very soon," he said.

Gan inserted a key into what appeared to be a very ordinary door. As he turned the key a narrow stairway leading down was revealed behind a recessed panel.

"There are a few things I need to brief you on. I thought we had more time, but it seems Marks and his boss want you out of the equation," said Gan.

They walked down the stairs to a state of the art medical facility bustling with activity.

"What is this place?"

The surprise was clear in her voice.

"This place is the one of the facilities used by the Grey," said Gan.

"The Grey?" *I thought that is just a rumor told to hunters to keep them in line?*

"The Grey is real?"

"As real as it gets, Blue. When things go south, we hunt the hunters," said Gan as he headed down a corridor with Sepia in tow. "Now let's get those chains off of you and find your gunman."

They wound through several corridors turning enough times that Sepia almost lost her bearings. At the end of one of the corridors they reached a large vault door. Gan put his hand on the panel next to the door and it whispered open. Inside stood one of the largest men Sepia had ever seen. His entire upper body was covered in intricate designs. Some of them resembled Sepia's own ink. His white hair was drawn back in a ponytail that ran down his back. His upper body was barely covered by the overalls he wore.

"Is that some kind of renegade brute?" Sepia whispered to Gan under her breath.

"Be polite. You do remember how to do that, right?"

"This must be the armory," she said as she looked around at the assembled weapons.

Every wall was covered with them. There were several workbenches, each with weapons in several states of assembly. She saw batons, sticks, rifles, handguns and every kind of edged weapon. Some she recognized, many she didn't.

The large man was sitting at one of the benches working on what appeared to be a large sword. He didn't look up as they entered.

"No, I am not some kid of renegade brute," he said as he remained focused on the work before him.

Sepia gave Gan a sidelong glance, cocking one eyebrow.

"Although I have been called worse," said the hunched figure.

He looked up then and Sepia saw the large scar that ran down one side of his rugged, weatherworn face. He looked like a grizzled grandfather.

Sepia walked up to the man and extended a hand, chains rattling.

"Sepia," she said. He was slightly taller than her, even while sitting.

"You're right, she is bold," he said as he wiped his hands on the front of his overalls.

"This is Hep, our weapons master. If it's made to kill, maim, or destroy, Hep will know how to use it."

Hep took Sepia's hand and shook it. His grip was a vise. *He is as strong as a brute.*

"Pleasure. Those are some interesting bracelets you got there," said Hep.

"Can you take them off?"

Hep grabbed the end of the chain and inspected it.

"These are hunter restraints. How did you manage to break them?" Hep said in disbelief.

"I pulled?" she said matter-of-factly.

He looked at her with new found respect and nodded. Hep examined the chain again.

"It wasn't the chain that gave but the bolt that held it. You shouldn't have been able to pull it free. Why were you in hunter restraints?"

The door opened again and a young man came in and whispered to Gan out of earshot for Sepia. She looked at Hep.

"Boring administrative duties, but he has to go," said Hep, showing that he had heard the man. The young man turned to face Hep, red-faced.

"Stop scaring the staff, get those chains off of her and check her sword. She is having problems aligning, so see if you can help," said Gan.

Gan walked out of the Armory following the young man as the door closed behind him. Sepia turned back to Hep and lifted both wrists.

"I have just the thing," he said as he fished in one of his toolboxes.

"How can you hear so well?"

"You mean even though he was trying to whisper? They all do it when they come here, to test me," said Hep as he chuckled.

"Yes, you heard me too, didn't you," said Sepia.

"Clear as a bell. It's my ink. My mother was an Inkmaster. Most of these designs protect me and give me affinity to elements, specifically metals. In a room like this"--he swept his arm around-- "all of my senses are heightened."

He kept looking in his tool box until he pulled out what looked like a thin metal straw.

"Okay, hold still, this is a laser pointer. As in a laser pointer that will remove your hand from your body if you shift at the wrong time. Understand?" Hep said, all trace of humor gone.

"Don't you have some kind of bolt cutters or something less limb-removing?" Sepia looked at the laser pointer with distrust. "How steady is your aim?"

"Bolt cutters won't work on these restraints," he said.

"Bolt cutters would make me feel better," said Sepia.

"This requires finesse, and don't worry I've done this a few times and it almost always works."

"Almost always?"

Hep smiled at her and grabbed her wrist as he hooked a stool closer with his foot.

"Sit down and don't move," he said.

She sat perfectly still. Moments later the chains were off and he had stored them in a special lock box.

"I'll keep these here for you in case you ever need them. Now hand me your sword," he said as he stood.

"I don't think that's such a good idea, Hep."

"You aren't aligning, so I need to see if it's a problem with the blade or you, or both," explained Hep.

Sepia undid the straps that held the scabbard in place and handed it over to Hep.

Hep pulled out Perdition and Sepia winced, expecting the worst. Hep laughed at her expression.

"It's not going to do anything to me. Who do you think repairs the hunters' swords when they need it?" He pointed to the designs across his chest. "So, why were you in restraints?"

"Honestly, I don't know. One moment I was dropping off Cade and the next I was getting tazed by some creep in a suit. He goes by the name of Marks, second in command to the Overseer South."

Hep gave a low whistle. "That guy is bad news, dangerous too. Gan has been watching him for some time now."

Hep went back to Sepia's sword. He held it and took some practice swings and then held it still again with his eyes closed.

"The energy of it is off balance somehow, you haven't been using it, is that right?"

Sepia looked away. "Not really, no," she said.

He turned it over and held it in his hand by the blade proper. He read the engraving on the blade. His eyes opened wide as he continued reading.

"This is Emiko's blade, Perdition. Shit, I didn't think they gave this to anyone else after what happened to her."

He put it on the bench reverentially, careful not to touch the edges.

"She was my mom, what happened to her? How did you know its name?"

"Your mom? Well that makes sense. Gan didn't tell you about her? Now I see the resemblance, well except for the--" He motioned at her eyes as he rubbed his chin.

"Not much. She was killed when I was very young, fighting a Nightmare, a T8," said Sepia.

"Well, technically that is true," he paused as he considered his next words. *What isn't he telling me?* she thought.

"I think I'll let Gan handle that one." She could see he wasn't going to say more on the subject.

"As for my knowing the name… Two ways:" He held up two meaty fingers.

They looked like huge sausages to Sepia. "Are you sure you aren't part brute?"

He narrowed his eyes at her in mock seriousness. He lifted the sword from the table and showed it to her.

"Pay attention. One, the metal speaks to me-- that is the only way I can describe it. Two, it's written there on the blade, see?"

He pointed to several of the inscriptions etched into the blade.

Sepia looked and only saw the characters she always saw, illegible to her.

"You can't read it?"

Sepia shook her head and Hep grew pensive.

"That is a problem. I can only read the name, because as a smith I have to know which blade I am working on, but the rest is hidden, even from me. That part is meant for you, the owner of the blade."

"So it's not the blade."

She had really hoped it was the blade, but knew in her gut it was her. Hep placed Perdition on the workbench and looked it over again, scrutinizing every inch.

"Well, physically the blade is perfect. It's designed in a hybrid katana fashion. You won't see another like it. The balance is perfect, and the edge is insane. This thing can slice air. Only named blades are like this. I never really have to work on the blades themselves just the other parts."

"That means I'm the problem," said Sepia

"Not necessarily. It could be a matter of aligning the blade, but--"

"But what?" Sepia said as a glimmer of hope crept into her voice.

"Well, it's your mom's blade. The assumption is that you would be the best candidate for it to align to, unless..."

"Unless what?"

"Well, a hunter's blade can only align to one person at a time. If it's not you, then the only other reason is that it's still bonded to its previous owner."

"That would mean--my mom?"

"--Is alive and out there somewhere. The blade senses it and rejects you on the deepest level."

Gan wouldn't lie to me, would he?

"There is a way to find out. If it's you, that is," said Hep.

"How do we do that?"

"The oldest and best way: we need to fight," said Hep as he grabbed a large broadsword from the wall and hefted it in his hands.

TWELVE

MARKS HEADED BACK TO HOME. The morning sun blazed in his eyes, signaling the start of the day for most and the end of one for him. Being on an unsanctioned location was not the issue for him. No one would know he was there. *How the hell did the Unholy find her and before I could follow through with my plan?*

He entered his office and checked his messages. Most of them were from Peterson. He would have to deal with him eventually. The first priority was eliminating Sepia. Taking over Manhattan South would happen, eventually. The elements were in place and it was only a matter of time. One of his assistants knocked on the door and entered. He forgot her name. They were all the same, nameless and faceless, tools to be used.

"Sir, Mr. Peterson would like to see you," she said.

I'm sure he would. "Thank you, I will be there shortly, I just need to prepare this document. Please inform him I will be in his office in five minutes," said Marks.

"Yes, sir," she said as she left his office.

Five minutes later he was standing before Magnus Peterson, listening to the man rant.

"One of the off-sites was active last night. Do you know anything about this?"

Marks looked down at his tablet and tapped it a few times. "That site was being used to store some volatile chemicals. It appears something went wrong with the storage facility within the site, sir."

"Make sure it's taken care of. I want no repercussions from Regional about this," said Magnus.

"Yes, sir. Is there anything else?" Marks was anxious to find Sepia.

"Yes, I read the report you provided me. Where is this hunter, Sepia Blue? What kind of name is Sepia Blue?" Magnus said.

That is a good question, thought Marks. *It certainly isn't her given name, what is she hiding?*

"Currently her whereabouts are unknown, sir."

"Excuse me? How can we not know where she is? Isn't she one of our hunters?"

"Yes, sir. It would appear she has problems following procedure," said Marks.

"I read that in the report. Bring her in, I would like to speak to her," said Magnus.

"Yes, sir. Any particular time frame sir?"

"Yes, I want her here yesterday. Is that immediate enough? Oh, and if she fails to comply, convince her."

"Yes, sir," said Marks.

This was a problem. He couldn't let Sepia meet Peterson, since it would unravel his plan. Too many questions would be asked, the wrong kinds of questions. He would have to find a solution. He looked down at his tablet and tapped its face several times. A solution presented itself.

"Sir, it says here they would like your presence at the off-site location to assess the damage."

"What, today? I have enough to worry about," said Magnus.

"I could go in your place, sir, even though it requests you be there," said Marks.

"No, I'd better go, if not I won't hear the end of it. Get a car ready and we can leave in an hour. Let me just take care of some matters here," said Magnus.

"Yes, sir," said Marks.

In an hour, Magnus Peterson would perform his last official act as an Overseer of the Order.

THIRTEEN

BEHIND THE WORKSHOP HEP had a firing range and an open area Sepia assumed was for sparring practice.

It was a wooden floor covered with sand and sawdust making for uncertain footing. In certain places she could see small rocks strewn about.

"Why the sand and rocks? This place is a broken ankle waiting to happen."

"This area is designed to be difficult to fight in. Sometimes I need to test out certain weapons. Some of the hunters help me out and we spar from time to time. The uncertain footing gives them a fighting chance." Hep smiled.

"Hunters know about this place?" Sepia said as she made her way around the floor.

"No, not all of them, they need to be a class two or higher and then only the ones Gan trusts, which aren't many. I don't get nearly as much practice as I would like," said Hep.

"So how is this supposed to work?"

"Named blades work on a simple principle. The metal is imbued with power, and that's what the inscriptions are for."

"Okay that part I knew. Each blade has a power given to it, which is tied to its name," she said.

"Exactly, and the other part is that the blade has to bond to its owner. That usually happens on the night a hunter is recognized."

Sepia gave Hep a blank stare.

"On the night you were given your blade? Didn't anything happen to you, something special?"

"No, not really. I was given the blade and was declared a hunter," said Sepia.

"Well, it's not unheard of. Sometimes it takes a few days, even a month."

"Hep, I've been a hunter for close to five years now," said Sepia.

"Maybe you're a late bloomer? Well, the other way to create the bond is under extreme duress. The hunter has to be in a life-threatening situation and the blade bonds to preserve the hunter."

"I've had those as well. It's not all roses and sunshine when I'm on patrol. Facing a T6 isn't enough duress?"

"Did you feel your life was in danger? I mean real danger, like it was you or the Nightmare."

She thought back to the last incident. Yes, she was scared, but she never felt like her life was in danger. Besides, Cade was there and she knew he would always have her back.

"No, it didn't feel that way. I was scared, but Cade was there and I just knew we would come out of it okay."

"How often have you used the blade in the years you have been patrolling?"

"I try not to. The last time was the fifth time I drew the blade in a fight, because I had to."

Hep gave her a long, hard stare.

"Are you saying that in five years you only drew your blade five times?"

"Yes, bad things happen when I use it. Bad things to others and especially me," said Sepia.

"That might be the problem. It may not be that your mom is alive, sorry about that, but that the bond it shared with her is stronger than the one it has with you. Basically the blade doesn't know you."

Sepia looked at him and held her blade. The broadsword he was leaning on was almost as tall as she was. Her blade looked like a toothpick in comparison.

"What are you saying? It's alive?"

She looked at the blade in her hand and could sense the power coursing through it, calling to her. The darkness was there, waiting.

"Not in the strict sense of life. It's not alive or sentient or anything like that."

"Then what?" Sepia said, exasperated.

 He could tell she was frustrated by this situation.

How do I explain this? "Okay, you see this sword?" he said as he waved the broadsword around with one hand.

"I can't really miss it, that thing is longer than me," she said as she backed up.

Hep chuckled. "As excellent a blade as this is, it's just a blade to me. It's just a piece of metal. I can use it and I'm actually very good with a blade this size, but I don't feel connected to it. It's not a part of me. A named blade becomes an extension of you, of your body, but it goes beyond that."

She thought she understood what he meant, that familiar feeling she got when she strapped it on. When she held it before it turned dark, it was a connection that ran deep into her core.

"I think I know what you mean," she said.

"When a hunter uses a named blade they are pretty much unstoppable. It's why there are no more than ten named blades active at any given time. Plus those who have named blades don't know which hunter has one," said Hep.

"Why? What's the big deal?"

"Think about it: If those ten decided it was time to take over the Order, who could stop them? I mean besides the Grey."

"So that's what the Grey is for? It's like an internal police force that no one knows exists?" said Sepia as she thought out loud.

"Yes, it's that kind of thing, of who watches the watchers," said Hep. "Or in this case, who hunts the hunters."

"What about the other hunters and rogues? Couldn't they stop the named blades?" she said.

"They could slow them down. Maybe take one or two, but not all ten," said Hep.

"Do you know why we aren't supposed to let anyone know their names? Doesn't make sense to me," said Sepia.

"Aside from creating an unstoppable force of hunters you mean? Names have power. There was a rumor of a nameless blade that could control all the named blades as long as the wielder knew the names," said Hep.

"Has that been done?"

"No one has ever found that blade. I think it's just another one of those rumors in the Order."

"Do you know the names of the blades?" said Sepia.

"I'll tell you what. If you beat me, I'll tell you all twenty names," said Hep

"Twenty? I thought you said there were only ten?"

"I said there were only ten active at any time. The other ten are stored in a vault at Home. Each blade is twinned to its opposite. Whichever blade is active, its twin is in storage, as a failsafe."

He faced her and assumed a fighting stance.

"Let's get you aligned," said Hep as he began to circle her.

Sepia took a defensive stance.

"I don't think this is going to work. It's not like you're going to--"

Hep slashed toward her. If her blade were not drawn he would have cut her in two. Only her reflexes saved her. She pushed off the broadsword and jumped back.

"What the hell, Hep?"

Her sword was still ringing from the clash of blades. He buried the tip of his sword in the sand on the floor.

"I told you, in order for the alignment to take place you need to feel that your life is in danger."

She sensed his attitude shift and felt the menace in the air. "You wouldn't be the first to die on this floor," he admitted.

He flicked up the tip of the sword, sending sand flying at her face. She raised her arm to protect her eyes while rotating her body clockwise. Hep lunged, aiming for her abdomen. The broadsword cut into her side, drawing blood.

"Shit, Hep," she said looking down to see the wound closing as the ink flared around the wound.

"Are we serious yet? Or do you think you can just dance around all my attacks?" Hep said, menace in his voice.

"I don't want to hurt you-- you don't understand what happens."

"That is the reason why you are at best a mediocre hunter," said Hep as he lashed out with a side kick.

Sepia dodged the kick, stepping in as she delivered a punishing elbow strike into his ribs. Her strike bounced off his side as she winced. He delivered an uppercut that lifted her off her feet and landed her several feet away on her back.

"That was a good shot, I almost felt that," he said as he rubbed his side.

With her sword pointed at Hep, she stood slowly.

"You have no idea what you are facing," said Sepia.

Hep spat to one side and flexed his massive arms as he raised the broadsword to one side of his body.

"Stop telling me and show me."

"Just remember, I warned you."

Sepia let the power envelope her. As she did, the blade of the sword grew darker. The inscriptions flared red and vanished beneath the inky black covering. Sepia began to smile as the dark aura crept over the blade and enveloped her arms.

Hep crouched "Well, hell yes, now we have a fight. Let's see what you got, little hunter."

Sepia ran at Hep. He began to bring his sword down in a crushing arc. Before she entered the death arc of the broadsword she leapt and flipped over Hep, landing behind him. Her blade bit into his back as he brought his fist behind, slamming her in the face and sending her sliding across the floor.

She wiped her face, leaving a trail of blood across her chin. Her ink would heal it eventually but it was slower on the parts not covered by the designs. Hep came in with a horizontal slash and changed trajectory mid slash aiming for her calves. Sepia avoided the slash and turned into his attack, slicing Hep's inner thigh while gracefully jumping over his leg. He fell to one knee as she circled him.

"Damn, that stings. You have to control the blade, Sepia, not the other way around," said Hep.

"I only see your blood on the floor."

His words barely registered. She noticed that he was healing fast and that she would need to cut him again and again if she were to kill him and be safe. Hep reached behind him and pulled out a dagger and smiled.

"I want you to know that I'm really enjoying myself. I haven't had this much fun well, since ever," said Hep.

Hep slid into her and body-checked her with his sword edge-first, cutting her arms with the dagger as she put up a defensive cross guard. The bracelet she wore on her wrist shattered from the dagger slashes. Using his sword like a staff, he smacked her in the face with the hilt, grabbing the blade as he swung his sword down. The pommel, which had sharpened hooks on either end, jammed into her thigh, tearing flesh. She was trapped against him and couldn't use her sword.

"You have to concentrate, Sepia, past the pain. Bring the sword to you. You control it-- not the other way around," he said as she struggled to get free.

He brought down the dagger and shattered her collarbone. She cried out then. Her arm hung at her side, useless. She was taking damage faster than her body could repair. Raising a leg she managed to kick the inside of his knee. It would have been shattered, but he saw it coming and moved. Turning his body he took the kick to the back of the leg, and it forced him to let her go to keep his balance. She backed up slowly, her eyes still focused on her enemy.

"I don't think you have what it takes, hunter. This has been a good exercise, but it will be better for everyone if I end you here," said Hep.

His tone left no doubt, he was going to kill her.

They circled for several seconds, each filled with cuts and bruises that were slowly healing. He drew back his sword and came running at her.

I will not die here, she thought. With her will, she reached in and grabbed the power that was coursing through and around her. The change was instant. Time slowed to a crawl. The black energy enveloping her blade and arms dissipated, revealing her blade and the inscriptions that were now a subtle green. The clarity of her senses bombarded her. She could feel the sand beneath her feet, and the sweat on her brow. She sensed the weight differential of Hep running as the vibrations reached her. Each vibration was a world of possibility, shifting points of attack, vectors and angles to be exploited. The information was reaching her through her blade. She had bonded with her sword.

He stepped in to deliver the killing blow. As she watched him move, it looked so slow. It would be so easy to avoid now. She saw his moves and the potential moves he could make, anticipating each outcome with a response. Each one was clear to her. She shifted her weight to avoid the deadly attack and was about to disarm Hep when he went flying back across the floor as if he had reached the end of a tether and was yanked back. The next moment Gan was in her face.

"What the hell is going on?" Gan said, furious.

Sepia had never seen him this angry. She looked down and noticed his hands were smoldering.

"I, we--" she stammered.

Hep was laughing in the corner. Gan turned to face him.

"Ow, ow that hurts!" Hep said between chuckles as he moved his arms and felt his chest tenderly. A palm print was faintly visible.

"That's got to be at least one, no, two broken ribs, ow. Let's see if it was worth it."

He stepped slowly over to Sepia who was still standing in the same place.

"Well? I saw the blade change and on my last run you looked totally different. I was a little concerned for my well-being," said Hep, smiling.

"I was able to pull it all back. All the power and the energy, I brought it back and it made everything so, clear," said Sepia. Hep was nodding as he stretched his arms, feeling for any more tender areas.

"I told you she was having problems aligning and I come here to find you attacking her. Explain, and make it convincing," said Gan.

"She bonded with her blade," said Hep.

Gan turned suddenly and looked at Sepia. "Is that true?"

Sepia nodded as she looked at her blade with new eyes, it seemed. She looked at the inscription and for the first time the symbols were clear to her and then she understood what she truly held in her hands.

"What does it say?" Hep said as he walked over to where she stood.

"The wielder of this blade commands the power of Perdition, twin to Salvation. Death and destruction, life and creation, as you reap so shall you sow," whispered Sepia.

Hep whistled low. "Now that is some serious mojo, right there. Do you feel different?"

"I don't know. Faster and stronger maybe, my senses seem to be on overdrive," said Sepia.

"You'll get used to it now that you're aligned. That does mean that your mom…" said Hep.

"Isn't alive out there somewhere, I know," said Sepia.

Hep nodded as he picked up his broadsword and walked over to the work area followed by Gan and Sepia. He placed both the dagger and the sword on the bench and sat down. He tossed one last item on the table and looked at Gan.

"Is this how you knew?"

Gan looked down at the last item. It was the bracelet he had given Sepia long ago, now broken.

"Yes, once it was destroyed I knew right away she was in danger," said Gan. "I didn't think that danger would be in the form of my weapons master."

"You do realize that those gems could have contributed to her being out of alignment?"

"No, I didn't think they would inhibit her ability to align," said Gan as he turned to Sepia. "I could have gotten you killed, I'm sorry."

"They seem to be more trouble than they're worth, Gan, I'll work on something similar that shouldn't interfere with her abilities," said Hep. "I'm guessing you have an intact bracelet?"

Gan gave it to him.

Sepia sheathed her sword and hugged Gan who had been the only father she ever knew.

"I know why you did it, but I'm a big girl now. Besides, I'm not out there alone you know," said Sepia.

"Speaking of which, Cade should be here any minute. I have to admit I may have given him reason to believe you were in danger," said Gan.

Cade came running into the armory with his gun drawn, looking around for Sepia.

"Sepia, you're okay? That old man can run," Cade said as he pointed at Gan.

She was glad to see Cade up and moving.

"I'm fine, what about you? Are you done lazing about?"

"I'm one-hundred percent. I'm ready to take names and kick ass."

Cade holstered his gun and began to look around, whistling low and long.

"Now this is what I call a candy store," said Cade.

Hep walked over to him and began to show him the weapons. Cade began asking about the rifles on the wall, grabbed several and headed to the range with Hep.

"I need you to stay here with Cade while he finishes recovering," said Gan. "You could do with some rest too."

"Where are you going? Does this have to do with the breaches?" Sepia said looking at Gan with concern.

"I have intel that the Overseer is going to do an assessment on the off-site location you were at last night," said Gan.

"The Overseer? Why would he go to an off-site?"

"Something about assessing the damage, but I think it's a setup, since it makes no sense for him to be there," said Gan.

"The guy I met, Jonathan Marks, is his second. He was the one asking the questions. Will he be there?"

"On something this delicate the Overseer doesn't travel without his second," said Gan.

The implication was clear and Sepia wanted to pay that son of a bitch back.

"Under no circumstances are you to go to that site. It will be crawling with the Overseer's men and I still don't know if he was behind your abduction or if was just Marks, acting alone."

"Fine, I'll need to figure out this alignment thing with Hep, anyway," said Sepia.

"I should be back by nightfall. I will know more by then and I can bring you up to speed," said Gan.

She nodded and Cade came up to them as Gan was turning to leave. "Where are we going?" said Cade.

"Nowhere. You stay here and recover. I need to get some information," said Gan over his shoulder.

They both looked at Gan who was walking toward the door. Gan stopped and turned around.

"Hep, make sure they do not leave this facility. I will hold you personally responsible if they do," said Gan.

Several assistants were waiting for Gan as he left the armory. Sepia turned to face Hep.

"You're going, aren't you?' said Hep.

"I can't let him go alone. Anyone he takes with him won't be a match for Marks. I have to make sure he returns in one piece," said Sepia.

"I won't even pretend I can stop you. Him, on the other hand I can stop." Hep pointed at Cade. "But I'm guessing you want him to go with you."

Sepia nodded.

"You're going to need this," said Hep as he walked over to the rifle rack and pulled off a long matte black rifle. Cade's eyes widened.

"That is a modified Barrett M50. Try not to break it," said Hep.

Cade took the rifle and smiled at Hep.

"Happy birthday and Merry Christmas to me," said Cade as he examined the weapon.

"You may need these," said Hep.

Hep handed her four daggers like the dagger he had used earlier. "It's good steel, not as good as your blade, but in a pinch, it's better than nothing."

She strapped the daggers to her thighs, replacing the ones Marks had taken.

"Thank you," said Sepia and she gave him a hug, which took him by surprise.

"Anytime, little hunter, you hurry back and we'll discuss named blades and maybe dance again." said Hep.

"That's a date, grandpa," she said as she walked out. Cade stood watching the interchange between them and scratched his chin.

"I'm out for a little a while and you go flirting with the first guy you meet?" said Cade as he ran to catch up to Sepia. She ignored him and kept walking, her pace fast.

"Cade?" Hep called out to him as he turned to catch up with Sepia. Cade turned back.

"Keep her alive, gunman."

Cade nodded, held up the rifle and broke into a jog to catch Sepia. Hep closed the door to the armory and hoped he would see her again soon. It had been several decades since he had encountered anyone as skilled or fearsome. She was very much her mother's daughter. He could only hope she would not share her mother's fate.

"Watch over them, Emiko," he whispered as he returned to his workbench.

FOURTEEN

HALF OF THE BUILDING WAS a burnt out husk. Marks could see from a distance that the structural integrity of the site was in danger. *Perfect for an accident,* he thought.

He drove up to the lot that faced the building and turned off the SUV.

"Is it possible we can just assess from here, sir? It looks like it's going to come down any moment," said Marks.

"What are you afraid of, Marks? We need to go in and look at the damage," said Magnus.

Several more SUVs approached the lot and set up a perimeter. Marks walked over to the drivers and began giving them instructions. Teams of men from the Order began fanning out among the debris.

"The men will begin the forensic investigation and find out the cause of this, sir," said Marks.

"Good. Let's go see what kind of damage was done to the building," said Magnus.

"Is that really necessary? I think it would be safer if you waited in the vehicle, sir."

"When Regional asks if I saw the site, I want to be able to describe it, Marks. Let's go in."

They walked into the ruined side of the building. Most of the actual structure appeared undamaged. The interrogation area was unrecognizable.

As they walked into the building Magnus began looking around.

"I thought you said this was a storage problem?"

"Yes, sir, that's what the report said," said Marks.

"Then why is the damage localized to this area, the holding cells. Why were we keeping volatile chemicals in this area?" said Magnus.

"I can answer that," said Gan.

He stepped out from the shadows with his gun drawn. Magnus looked confused. Marks turned to face Gan and put his hands up.

"Hello, Gan. I have to say I'm surprised to see you here," said Marks.

"Who is this? Marks, do you know this man?"

"So it was you after all. You were the one who kidnapped Sepia," said Gan.

"You did what?" said Magnus.

"Sepia and I have some unresolved business, old man," said Marks.

"That's going to be a problem. I'm here to make sure you leave her alone," said Gan.

"That hunter is a renegade and needs to be debriefed. She clearly violates procedure and will be suspended pending an investigation," said Magnus.

Both Gan and Marks looked at Magnus. Gan spoke first.

"An investigation? He isn't planning an investigation," said Gan as he pointed the gun at Marks. "He was planning an execution."

"Ridiculous. I gave no such order. She was to be brought Home where I would…" Magnus looked down at his chest where two small red circles blossomed into pools. He turned to look at Marks.

"You…shot…me?" Magnus said as he collapsed to the ground.

"And still he doesn't shut up," said Marks. He held a standard issue Order pistol in his hand. It was very similar to what Gan held. Gan looked down at Marks' gun. *When the hell did he draw that? He's fast.* Marks began removing the silencer from his gun.

"He was going to have a fatal accident in here, but this is even better. You, angered at being retired early decided to take vengeance on the Overseer, shooting and killing him. I returned fire, but was too late to save him," said Marks.

Gan was moving as Marks shot several times, hitting him once in the arm and throwing him off balance. Gan threw himself out one of the side windows and began to run to the main complex. Overseer agents rushed into the building surrounding Marks.

"Sir, are you okay?" said one of the lead agents.

"He shot the Overseer! Get him!" Marks yelled as he knelt over the body of Magnus.

The agents began to pursue Gan.

Looking through his scope, Cade could see the activity.

"Shots fired, Blue. It looks like Gan was hit."

"Goddammit, where is he hit?"

"Looks like the arm, not fatal but he's losing a lot of blood," said Cade.

Sepia looked over the side of the roof and jumped down, landing on an adjacent roof and tucking into a roll. She ran an intercept path hoping to get to Gan before the Order agents did.

"What the hell was he thinking going in there alone?" she said. "How many agents are on the ground, Cade?"

Cade's voice came in over her com.

"I'm counting ten on him, you'd better hurry since they will cut him off quick," said Cade.

"Get the truck and bring it to the corner. I'll be coming in hot," she said.

"See you in two," said Cade as he jumped off the roof and ran to their truck. He put it in gear and sped off to her location.

"Change of plans, Cade. He ran into the main complex. We're coming out the south side."

Cade turned the wheel as swerved around taking the truck to the far end of the facility.

"Got it, make this fast, Sepia. They looked pretty pissed," said Cade.

"Why, why did you do this?" said Magnus between breaths.

They were alone as the agents pursued Gan. Marks made sure of it. He looked down at Magnus as he held his head.

"It's time for you to retire, Magnus. The Order needs change. This is only the first step, in time I will control the Order."

"You're crazy, there's no way you can do this alone," said Magnus.

"Who says I'm alone? Besides, no one listens to the man who is dying. Don't worry, it's not your concern any longer," said Marks.

He placed a hand over Magnus's face and made sure he breathed his last. Several agents came in to report.

"Take his body to the vehicle. Has the assassin been caught yet?" said Marks.

"No, sir," said one of the agents.

"Then what the hell are you doing here? Forget the body, I'll do it. Join the others and bring me the man responsible for this!" Marks said as he pointed down to Magnus.

"Yes, sir!" The two agents ran off to join the pursuit.

Marks removed the specialized key card from Magnus's jacket and placed it in his pocket. He bent over and lifted Magnus's body and stepped outside to the vehicle placing the body in the back and waited.

Gan was getting dizzy from the blood loss.

"There he is!" the voices came from everywhere.

Gan could hear the agent voices behind him. The building complex was immense, but it would do him no good if he couldn't put distance between them. He dashed into one of the rooms and stopped. Getting his bearings he realized he would be surrounded soon. *Talk about amateur hour. This is bad.* He wrapped the arm to stop the bleeding hoping it would buy him time.

Sepia entered the complex and took a deep calming breath. She slid quietly into one of the rooms and listened. They still didn't know where Gan was, which was good. The bad part was she didn't know where he was either. *I need to practice my geolocation,* she thought. She saw an agent approach her doorway and hugged the wall. As he walked by she grabbed him in a choke hold and put him to sleep. Walking down the corridor she imagined where Gan would go when she heard a shuffle in one of the rooms. She stopped midstride and so did the shuffle. She peered in to the room where she heard the noise and jerked her head back instinctively. A fraction of a second later and Gan would have broken her neck.

"Gan," she whispered. He collapsed into her arms. His face was pale from the blood loss.

"Cade, I'm coming out. Prep a med kit, he's in bad shape," said Sepia.

"Prepped and waiting, better make your move now. You have more heading your way," said Cade.

Cade saw more trucks arrive on the lot, agents spilling out of them and approaching the main building.

She peeked out the doorway to make sure it was empty. Holding Gan in a fireman's carry, she ran for the back door. She made it three steps before the first bullet ripped into her thigh.

"Over here!" said the agent. She could hear the footfalls of the other agents rushing to her location. The flush of heat let her know that her ink was taking care of the injury. She kept running despite the pain shooting up her leg. She fell into the back of the truck with Gan. Cade took off as she slammed down the rear door, bullets ricocheting off the reinforced steel.

The lead agent headed to the SUV where Marks stood.

"Sir, he managed to get away," the lead agent said.

"How did that happen?" said Marks.

"He had help, sir. The hunter that was here last night," said the agent. Marks could see the man was observant.

"What's your name, agent?"

"I'm Benson, sir. James Benson," replied the agent.

"Good, Benson, you are now point on this, I have to get back Home and deal with the death of our Overseer and the transition of office. I want you to find the assassin and the hunter who assisted him in this crime. I am holding you personally responsible for this, Benson. Do you understand me?"

"Yes, sir," said Benson.

Marks entered his SUV and drove away.

FIFTEEN

"CALISTO. YOU HAVE TO TAKE ME to Calisto," said Gan.

His voice was just above a whisper.

"You want us to go to 26th Street? Is she there?" said Sepia.

Gan was fading in and out of consciousness.

"Park. Go to the 59th and Columbus Circle entrance," said Gan

"The park. Are you sure, Gan? It will be dark soon," said Sepia.

"I can't compromise Grey, and can't go Home. Calisto is the best option," said Gan just before losing consciousness again.

"Cade, we need to go to the park."

"I heard him, but are you sure you want to do this?"

"If we don't he dies in the truck," she said.

"If we do, we may all die in the park. Who is this Calisto, anyway?"

"She's a friend, his friend at least. I think she can help him," said Sepia.

"The park it is, then," said Cade.

Cade accelerated the SUV as he went under the EL that carried the 7 train. Several moments later three more SUVs were behind them.

"We have company," said Sepia.

"I see them. I'm going to try and shake them. It's going to get bumpy back there so hold on."

Sepia did her best to secure Gan in the rear seat using the seat belts and jumped into the passenger seat next to Cade.

"These guys are persistent," said Cade.

He clenched his teeth as he made a sharp turn onto the bridge approach. Sepia lowered her window and began shooting at the tires of the pursuing SUVs.

"Can't you keep this thing still? I'm trying to get a shot off."

"You realize this is called evasive driving for a reason," he said as he swerved across two lanes and into Queens Plaza. The SUVs followed the maneuver. Sepia smacked her head against the side of the door and cursed under her breath.

"Sorry, but if we are going to make the park before they box us in I'm going to have to punch it."

Sepia rubbed her head. "Do what you need to do."

She kept shooting and managed to hit the passenger side tire of the lead van.

"I swear I hit that truck's tire," she said.

"Won't make much of a difference, since they are probably using run flats," he said.

"Shit. Everything else is bullet proof on those things," said Sepia.

"They're Order vehicles, it's the standard OP," said Cade.

"So we need to put some distance between us then," said Sepia.

"Let's see if we can buy ourselves some time. Hold on," warned Cade.

Cade swerved in to the outer roadway of the bridge, scraping the side of the truck. Sepia strapped in her seatbelt. The three trucks followed single file now.

"It's not going to be a straight shot to 59th now. This will lead us out to First Avenue," said Cade.

The lead truck rammed them from behind. Cade stepped on the gas pushing the truck even faster.

"At the bottom of the ramp don't take the turnaround, go straight to 61st and cut left," said Sepia. "What I wouldn't give for a rocket launcher right now."

They sped over the bridge, the Order trucks closing the distance.

"Hold on, this is going to be ugly," said Cade.

The bottom of the ramp forked into a hairpin turn which also led into a straightaway. There was no way to make the hairpin at their current velocity. At the last second Cade wrenched the wheel and turned right, slamming the left side of the truck into the wall as a method of stopping. Losing just enough momentum, he sped down the straightaway. The lead truck tried to mimic Cade's move but failed, slamming into the wall and totaling the vehicle. The next truck managed to make the turn and continued to pursue Cade.

"Make the left on Lex and take the right on 60th that will take us straight into the park," said Sepia.

"What the hell did he do? I've never seen the Order this determined to get someone."

"I don't know, but whatever it is they don't want him alive to talk about it."

Sepia looked back as she was arranging her weapons and tightening the straps. She moved into the back seat where Gan was and began to get him ready to move. *Don't you leave me, old man. You don't get to die today.* She grabbed Gan and pulled him to the front row.

"Cade, go right into the park." *I hope I'm right about this,* she thought. Cade swerved around a statue and drove right into the park destroying benches as he entered. The two trucks stopped outside of the park, and the agents jumped out weapons drawn.

Cade drove further in until he felt he was out of range from their guns.

The pursing SUVs reversed several hundred feet and came to a stop as Benson got out of the truck and called Marks.

"Sir, the assassin and the hunter got away," said Benson.

"Where are they now, Benson?"

"They have entered the park through the south exit near Columbus and 59th Street."

As expected, thought Marks.

"Do not pursue them into the park. Leave one team stationed at the exit. Gather the rest of your men and return Home," said Marks.

"But, sir, it's possible we can pursue," said Benson.

"The EMP field the park gives off will destroy all your electronics, and Benson do you think you are capable of being worse than whatever waits for them in the park?"

"No, sir, I just thought."

"That is not what you are paid to do. Gather your men and head back to Home, now," said Marks.

"Yes, sir," said Benson.

The Order has fulfilled on its word. Let's see if you keep yours, Marks thought as he hung up.

Cade stopped the truck and put it in park.

"Okay, now what? This is the proverbial jumping from the frying pan into the fire --except in this case the fire is a raging furnace."

"I know. Let me see if I can bring him to. I don't want to be here any longer than we have to be," said Sepia.

She cradled his head gently and called out to him.

"Gan, Gan? We're in the park, now how do we find Calisto?" said Sepia. In the distance she could hear the Unholy. They were coming. Gan opened his eyes and looked past Sepia.

"She knows I'm here. She always knows." He closed his eyes again but Sepia could see he remained conscious.

"How long, Gan? How long before she comes here?" she said.

The Unholy were getting closer. She hoped there weren't any Nightmares in the welcoming committee.

"I don't know, Blue. Trust me, she knows I'm here. When she comes depends on how pissed she is with me," said Gan.

"Do I even want to know, Gan? Why would she be angry with you?" said Sepia. Cade began prepping his rifle. "We have some activity, twelve o'clock."

Sepia looked out the front of the truck to see some of the Unholy approaching.

"Dreadwolves. I hate them. It's never just one with them," said Cade.

"Gan, what is the deal with you and Calisto?" Sepia checked her guns and extra magazines. She would go through them fast with Dreadwolves.

"We have a bit of history. Don't go out there with those wolves. We should be safe in here. Besides, I'm feeling better," said Gan. Sepia looked at him and the color had returned to his face, but the wound still looked bad.

"Gan, this is a vehicle designed to prevent small arms fire from penetrating. Not the Unholy. They will shred this truck like tissue paper. Stop avoiding the question," she said.

Cade had lowered a window and began shooting the Dreadwolves. As he had guessed, it was a pack.

"If you can get the pack leader they will usually run off," said Sepia.

"Found him, and he's hanging back. Probably waiting to see what's in here before coming down."

"See if you can wing him, usually that will send the pack running," said Sepia.

Cade slowed his breathing and aimed. He squeezed the trigger, his shot grazing the rear flank of the large Dreadwolf. The pack leader howled, its gray coat bristling. Then it growled and ran towards the truck.

"Or sometimes all it does its make the pack leader attack you," said Cade. The large gray wolf slammed into the driver's side of the truck, denting the door.

"Is she coming or should I just feed you to them, Gan?" Sepia said as the truck was rocked again.

"Fine. She's my wife," said Gan defeated.

"She's your *what*? You didn't think this was an important bit of information?"

"It's complicated, and you wouldn't understand," said Gan.

Cade started laughing. "We're all going to be dog food and you're afraid of your wife? Oh, that's priceless."

Another Dreadwolf rammed the truck. It would only be a matter of time before they attacked with their fangs. A few of the pack were gnawing on one of the tires. Cade reversed the truck to distract them before they shredded it.

"Electrical system is frying. If I turn it off it stays off. Even insulated we have maybe ten minutes before the EMP pulse destroys it."

The Dreadwolves had the truck surrounded when a high pitched whistle pierced the air. The wolves stood still as a figure came over the crest of the hill. The pack leader padded over to the figure and waited. The figure walked over to the pack leader, bent down and whispered something to the leader. The pack leader howled and the wolves began to disperse.

The smell of fresh cut grass filled the air. It was the smell of life, of vitality. For Sepia it was the smell of the first day of spring, full of promise.

"What is that smell? It reminds me of mowing the lawn when I was a kid," said Cade.

"That's her," said Gan.

Calisto, dressed in her usual attire looked at home in the park. Sepia opened the door and walked over to her.

"Hello, Hunter. I see you have found some measure of balance with your blade," said Calisto.

"Hello, Calisto. Gan is hurt and needs help," said Sepia.

Calisto cocked her head to one side. "Oh really, he does, does he?"

Gan exited the truck and made a show of walking around.

"I'm okay, really. I don't think it's going to get any worse." He took a few more steps before collapsing.

"Bring him. It's not safe here. Leave the truck running so it will serve as a distraction for the Unholy," said Calisto.

"Is there any place in here that is safe?" said Cade under his breath as he carried Gan.

"For your kind, no. But for me there are many safe havens even within the land of Nightmares," said Calisto as she led them away.

SIXTEEN

MORE THAN THREE DECADES had passed since the wards were weak enough for him to exit the pen they called their home. The time had drawn close to allow him to destroy the wards completely. All he needed was a named blade hunter foolish enough to enter the park. They were so close. His uneasy alliance with the Order was testing his patience.

"My Lord, there are intruders upon our grounds," said the minion. It was a misshapen creature that had been human once and now served the Nightmares, an Unholy.

"More curious humans, just let the Dreadwolves have them," said the Nightmare.

"These intruders are different, my Lord."

"In which way are they different?" said the Nightmare.

"Two males, one female, and the female is a hunter," said the minion.

"Where?"

"They are near the south edge of the grounds. One of the males is injured. They are with the witch," said the minion.

The Nightmare Lord's eyes narrowed as he looked down at the minion. The minion cowered under the gaze. No one could withstand that gaze for more than a few seconds. Each eye turned a different color as he looked at the creature at his feet.

"I tire of her interference," the Nightmare Lord said as he left the meeting chamber. *The Order is finally fulfilling its word. The plan is set and our time of captivity is drawing to a close.* For the first time in a long time, the Nightmare Lord began to smile.

"Locate them. Do not look for the hunter, since the witch will have her hidden. Look for the witch--if you find her, you find the hunter," said the Nightmare Lord.

"Yes, my Lord," said the minion, bowing.

****

Calisto led them through the Park taking several different paths. It was clear she was trying to prevent them from being followed.

"Why is this place so familiar to me?" said Sepia. Calisto spoke as they made their way through the forest.

"You don't remember? You used to come here often when you were a little girl, with your mother," said Calisto.

"My mom brought a child into the park?"

"You were a special child and your mother was not just a hunter."

"I bet," said Sepia.

They walked along a cobble stone path that wound around a small lake.

"This was just over thirty years ago. The park was different back then. Besides, your mother was a class one hunter, one of the twenty. Very few things in this park would confront her and those that could felt the price was too high," said Calisto.

"One of the twenty? Gan never told me that," said Sepia.

Sepia looked at his unconscious form. *I wonder what else he has kept from me?*

"If he didn't tell you, he must have his reasons," said Calisto as they headed over a stone bridge. They drew closer to a small building that was on the other side of the lake.

"Calisto, do you know how my mother died?" said Sepia.

Calisto nodded. "The hunters were losing against the Unholy. It was a period of chaos and the wards were failing, much like they are now. She helped stop a phalanx of behemoths and probably saved this city in the process. This happened at the location you call Bryant Park."

"Gan told me she took on a T8 alone. That it killed her," said Sepia.

Calisto looked at Gan and then back at Sepia as if weighing how much she should tell her.

"It's a little more complicated than that. Understand that a class one hunter is rare. In the entire history of the Order there are perhaps one hundred class one hunters recorded," said Calisto.

"So a T8 shouldn't have been a problem? Is that what you're saying?" said Sepia.

"I think I have said too much," said Calisto.

"Please, Calisto. I need to know," said Sepia.

"Gan is better suited for this, I'm not good with words, or sympathy," said Calisto. "But since he is indisposed, I will tell you. The reason a T8, as you call it, was able to defeat your mother was because she was betrayed."

"Betrayed, by who?" said Sepia.

"She was betrayed by her gunman. In the midst of the battle he shot her, wounding her. It was enough for the Nightmare to gain the advantage," said Calisto.

Sepia grew silent as they reached the building. The structure that appeared to be a small cottage from across the lake turned out to be a small keep.

"What the hell? From over there this place looked like a small outhouse," said Cade.

"That is one of the dangers of walking around here alone," said Calisto. "Things are rarely what they seem to be."

Calisto opened the door to the keep and led everyone inside. The door closed behind them sealing them from the park.

"This is your home?" said Sepia.

She looked around and despite the stone the space felt warm and inviting. The style of the interior was understated and minimal, with large rugs covering the stone floor and several paintings on the wall. Lamps hanging from the ceiling gave the room a warm glow.

"This is the Hunter's Keep. It belonged to your mother and other hunter's close to her level," said Calisto.

Cade gave a low whistle. "They kept a base inside the park? These hunters were badass," he said.

"Class one hunters are tasked with being a pre-emptive force. They stopped countless threats before anyone knew about them. As I said they were a formidable group and had little to fear in the park. The ground around the keep is warded and will deter most of the lower creatures," said Calisto.

Cade placed Gan down on one of the settees that were around the entryway. Two young men entered the foyer. They dressed Gan's wound and removed him.

"You can stay here for a few days. It will take some time before you draw attention to yourself. The keep itself is warded so you should remain hidden from most," said Calisto.

Sepia looked around at the men and women who were dressed in simple clothes going about several tasks.

"Who are they?" said Cade. He looked at the two until they were out of sight, taking note of the stairway they used at the rear of the foyer.

"They help here in the keep. Humans who entered the park and found themselves lost," said Calisto.

"You mean slaves. You kept them here?" said Sepia. Anger laced her words.

For a brief moment, anger flared in Calisto's eyes.

"Indignation does not suit you, hunter. Who is keeping who? Are we not in a large cage? Are the wards keeping others out or the Unholy--a human term for the denizens of the park-- in?"

Sepia, her face flushed in shame, couldn't answer.

"I'm sorry, but those people," said Sepia.

"They are here of their own free will since each was given the choice of leaving the park to return to their lives. They chose to stay here. Many of them were living on the streets, the usual prey for the Unholy," said Calisto.

Sepia looked around and could see more of the helpers cleaning or walking with purpose to attend to some duty. They looked happy despite living in the most dangerous area in the city.

"I guess this is an improvement over the streets," said Cade.

"It certainly is," said Calisto. She spoke to one of the women who approached.

"Martha here will show you to your rooms. Try and get some rest, since tomorrow will be a long day."

Martha led them through the corridors to their respective rooms where they both slept through the night. In the morning Martha knocked on their doors and led them to the dining room. Breakfast was on the table and Gan was already eating. Calisto was beside him and they were discussing something when Sepia and Cade walked in. They both grew silent while Sepia and Cade ate. Once breakfast was done Calisto stood, looking sidelong at Gan, she spoke to Sepia.

"Come, I doubt your arrival here was an accident or went unnoticed so we may as well make the most of it."

"What do you mean not an accident?" said Sepia.

"It was clear you were supposed to come here, to the park," said Calisto.

"How do you figure that?" said Cade.

"Tell me you trained them better than this, Gan. They can't possibly be this naïve," said Calisto.

Gan gave her a hard look and she softened a bit.

"You'll have to forgive me. I'm just not used to dealing with people. It's been a long time since I have had anyone to speak to, besides Ursa," she said. It was her turn to give Gan a hard look. He coughed and turned away. "Please come with me, we do have to prepare."

She began walking down one of the side corridors after speaking to one of the young girls.

"Prepare? Prepare for what?" said Sepia. They followed Calisto who moved at a fast pace.

"He will be coming, the one we call Chimera. He is a Nightmare Lord and surpasses any number you may have on a threat scale for those creatures." She stole a glance a Gan as she said this.

"And he knows we are here? How does he know this?" said Cade.

"I am certain he knows you are here but it will take some time before he can find you. How he knows is simple, even though he may be confined to the park, he has informants and spies outside," said Calisto as she took one corridor after the other. They entered a large training area. Gan came in after them.

"What is he, a brute? Something large? Just put me on the roof and I'll take him down," said Cade.

"With bullets? You intend to shoot it?" asked Calisto. "I'm afraid it will take more than that."

"All I need is one clean shot. One Nightmare, --lord or not, --I can drop him," said Cade as he tapped his rifle. Gan shook his head.

"Bullets won't stop this Nightmare, boy. Come with me and I'll show you how you can slow it down and maybe buy us a few seconds, maybe enough to save your sorry ass," said Gan.

Calisto took Sepia off to the other side of the training area.

"Let's begin. Draw your blade and align with it," said Calisto.

Sepia drew Perdition from its scabbard. Calisto clapped her hands together and slowly spread them apart, forming a blade from energy.

"What kind of blade is that?" asked Sepia.

"When you progress far enough you will be able to store your blade within you, eliminating the need for a scabbard," said Calisto. "Each hunter has a unique method of retrieval."

"Store it where?"

Calisto held her blade in her hand. Its steel gleamed with its own light.

"A blade is just another expression of energy. Like the matter around us. A named blade like yours will be easier to store once you learn how, but for now let's work on your alignment," said Calisto.

Four days passed in this way. Each day Calisto took Sepia to the training area to work on her blade alignment while Gan took Cade aside to work on the vulnerable aspects of targets and which weapons to use.

Now, on the fifth day the keep felt empty somehow. That morning Martha did not awaken Sepia, rather it was Calisto who came to her room.

"I'm afraid our time has come to a close. I have received news that Chimera will be on the move here soon. Unfortunately you are not ready to face him yet," said Calisto.

"I'm aligned now, don't you think I can handle him?" said Sepia.

"You aren't fully aligned. As you are now, he will kill you in short order. Being aligned is only the beginning. I have prepared a room to mask you, but you must leave through the tunnels. Gan and I will slow him down enough for you to get out of the park."

"Out of the park?"

Calisto nodded as she began moving. "It's the only way you will be safe. A word of caution, you cannot trust your fellow hunters, since the spy Chimera has must be among them or your organization, The Order. Treat everyone as a potential enemy."

Gan came around the corner with Cade and several bags of ammo and rifle parts. Falling in behind Calisto, Gan gave Cade some magazines.

"Remember you are not to engage this creature." Gan was speaking with Cade as they walked up.

"In this room is a hatch that leads to tunnels. These tunnels will take you to the west side of the park. Stay on the main artery and do not deviate from that. If you do you will get lost down there," said Gan. He and Cade looked at their watches and synced the time.

"Once I give you the signal you head down and jackrabbit through. Don't stop for anyone or anything, understand?" said Gan.

Calisto was walking deeper into the keep. It smelled musty and Sepia could see cobwebs across most of the corners.

"I got it, old man, are you coming with?"

"What did I just say? You don't wait for anyone. You keep going until you are out on the other side," said Gan.

Sepia could sense the fear in the air. "Is this Nightmare Lord really that powerful?"

Gan looked at Calisto. Sepia caught the nod he gave her. Calisto turned to Sepia.

"Every creature in park fears Chimera," said Calisto.

"Why is that?" said Sepia.

Calisto turned another corner and stood before a large reinforced door.

"In here, both of you. This room should mask you until you use the tunnels," said Calisto.

"Why, Calisto? What is it that they fear?" said Sepia.

Calisto was about to close the door, she turned and faced Sepia, sadness in her eyes.

"He is incredibly powerful, but he has one thing that sets him apart from all others."

"What?" said Sepia not really wanting to hear the answer.

"His eyes hunter, he has eyes just like yours," said Calisto.

Calisto closed the door and the room began to give off a low level hum.

Sepia felt like she just been gut-checked. The air rushed out of her lungs and she sat on the bed, stunned.

"Hey, so what it has eyes like yours? That proves nothing. You are still you. C'mon, let's get moving. Find the hatch, we need to be ready to go. Shake it off," said Cade.

Sepia snapped out of her reverie.

"Fine, I'll locate the hatch you get our things ready to move," said Sepia.

"That's what I just, -- never mind," said Cade.

"What is this signal Gan is going to give you?" said Sepia.

"He said we will feel a small earthquake and that will be our signal to haul ass."

"A small earthquake. You do realize this is still New York? We are sitting on bedrock," said Sepia.

She continued to search the floor for the hatch, without luck.

"Do you think they may have gotten the wrong room? I'm not seeing a hatch anywhere around here," she said.

"Take a breath and spread out, find the gap in the floor beneath us."

Why didn't I think of that? Sepia stood in the middle of the room and took several deep breaths. She let her senses spread out and felt under the floor in the upper right corner a depression.

"Found it!" said Sepia. She moved over to the corner and looked for a handle or latch to open the trapdoor. She felt around for a few moments and found the latch. Grabbing it with both hands, she pulled until the muscles in her arms bulged. Nothing happened for a moment and then she felt the rush of air as the trapdoor opened revealing a staircase.

"I can't believe there's a Nightmare out there powerful enough to scare Calisto. She helped train my mother; it means she has to have some skill. Did you see what she did with the sword?"

"Every day. That clap and 'pull the sword out of thin air' bit is impressive and scary as hell," said Cade.

"And yet this Nightmare is off the scale? Maybe we should stay and help?" Cade gave her a look.

"No, Blue. You know I always have your back, but we aren't staying," said Cade as he rubbed his hand through his hair. "Calisto looked pretty freaked out about this Chimera guy. We aren't sticking around to find out why."

Sepia stopped pacing and crossed her arms on her chest, glaring at Cade.

"Don't give me that look, Blue. You heard her. The thing is off the charts."

"Fine, how soon until we get this signal?" said Sepia.

"It should be any moment now according to Gan. This Chimera knows where we are, so he should be heading our way," said Cade.

"Maybe we can head out and then come back in, so we give it the impression we are escaping but we aren't," said Sepia.

Cade threw up his hands in frustration while mumbling under his breath. "Fine, fine, we want to go out and rush into the Nightmare that is going to crush us. Sure why not?"

"Okay, okay, we stick to the plan. I hate this. I hate running," said Sepia.

"Don't think of it as running, think of it as a strategic withdrawal. Let's go wait in the tunnel," he said.

Sepia glared at him as she descended the stairs. She began to feel a strange sensation across her skin. It felt like an immense buildup of static electricity.

"Cade, I can feel him getting closer," she said.

Cade started undoing the several grenades he kept on him. He assembled them to create a chain detonation for increased firepower.

"Let's make sure no one follows us down this tunnel," he said. He began to rig the grenades at the beams reinforcing the tunnel.

"The cross beams aren't the weak spots. Put the grenades there on the joists," said Sepia.

"This is not my first explosive adventure, Blue," he said.

He placed several grenades on each joist and tied the pins together with filament.

"Sorry, let's just get out of here," she said. They both headed down the tunnel as far as the filament would allow without pulling the pins.

Sepia could still feel the low thrum of power coursing through the room.

"Once I pull these, we run like there's no tomorrow, if not we get buried in here and this was all for nothing," said Cade.

Sepia remained silent clearly upset about leaving the park.

"I'm sorry about this, Blue, but this is the best way. We have to make sure you get safe," said Cade.

"What are you talking about? We're both getting out of here."

Cade side kicked Sepia, taking her off guard as she fell and rolled forward several feet. He rushed toward the grenade filled joists pulling all of the pins. Sepia had barely enough time to recover when the grenades went off.

"Cade, no! Cade, are you there?" The dust and the rubble made it impossible to see. She calmed her breathing and sensed him on the other side of the rubble heading back into the keep.

"Goddammit, Cade. You bastard!" she yelled. She started kicking at the rubble.

"Miss? We need to get ready to leave, Miss." It was Martha.

"What the hell are you doing here?" Sepia vented her frustration on the young girl.

"Mistress Calisto asked that I take you to the end of the tunnel, Miss," said Martha.

Martha no longer wore simple clothing. She was wearing rugged denim pants with several pockets, which covered black steel toed boots. A tight-fitting sweater with a shoulder holster held a large pistol.

"You were homeless?" said Sepia.

"Did a few tours in the desert, came home with PTSD. Couldn't hold a job, couldn't connect with my family. I found myself on the street drinking and doing drugs. One day I wandered in to the park to end it and Calisto found me. She helped me get clean, helped me find myself again."

"We need to get back to the keep," said Sepia as she removed stones.

"We need to go down the tunnel, Miss. Things are going to get real bad real fast. Let's go, please," said Martha. Sepia dropped the stones reluctantly. There was something in Martha's tone, fear.

"Fine, let's go. Someone had better have an answer for me," said Sepia under her breath.

****

Cade made it out of the tunnel in a cloud of dust. Gan grabbed him by the arm and hauled him up.

"Did you collapse it like we planned?" said Gan.

Cade was coughing and started removing the dust from his face.

"She's on the other side of the debris. I'm guessing Martha will take her the rest of the way?" Cade said between coughs.

"Martha is part of the Grey. She will take Sepia somewhere safe until we deal with this thing." Gan smiled. "Or it deals with us."

"You are having way too much fun, old man," said Cade, a grin on his face.

"You head upstairs. That Nightmare is still out there. I'll go see where Calisto is," said Gan.

Cade ran off looking for a stairwell that led to the roof. Gan headed for the foyer and front door, he could sense the Nightmare outside. His senses weren't as keen as a hunter's, but he learned to listen to his intuition long ago. It had saved his life too many times.

In the tunnel, Sepia stopped and began to head back. "I can't leave them."

Her arm was grabbed from behind. She swung around dagger in hand. Martha stopped her mid swing with a dagger of her own. Sepia could see she was trained and then it made sense.

"You're in the Grey, aren't you?" said Sepia.

Martha nodded. "That's why I'm down here with you. Gan said you would do this," said Martha.

"I almost cut you," said Sepia.

"Not likely. You may be a hunter but we aren't slouches in the Grey," said Martha. "Besides, I was trained by the same guy who trained you."

Sepia looked at her with newfound respect.

"Listen, you can't go out there and fight that thing not now, not yet. It's too strong. You and I need to get out of the park before it gets here," said Martha.

"No way, Martha, this thing is dangerous and I'm going to stop it," said Sepia.

"You still don't get it. This is not a T6 it's not even a T10. There is no number for the threat level it is. This thing is out of your league. You face it tonight, you will die," said Martha

"So I should leave them to face it alone? The only people I care about?"

"Yes if you care about them, like you say, you have to."

Sepia looked into her eyes and saw how serious she was. Martha was afraid.

"I can't," said Sepia. "I don't abandon my friends."

"It's not even close yet and you can sense it, what does that tell you?" said Martha.

Martha was right, Sepia's skin was electrified. She could see goose bumps running up and down her arms.

"That I'm getting better with my abilities?" said Sepia.

"Try again," said Martha.

It dawned on her that this was the first time she had ever sensed a Nightmare that wasn't close. The words came out with reluctance.

"That it's strong, too strong for me," said Sepia.

"These tunnels lead to the West Side. They agreed on you coming with me. Those are my orders to get you to a safe house. Cade, your gunman wasn't pleased with it either, but he agreed to the plan," said Martha.

"He wouldn't be, since he likes to watch my back," said Sepia.

"Then think of it as that. Right now they are watching your back. They are making sure you get safe," said Martha.

"Why would they do this?" said Sepia.

"If I had to guess I would say they care for you a great deal. Let's honor that by getting you safe," said Martha. Sepia nodded and they headed down the tunnel at a brisk pace.

"I'm sorry, I didn't know. I thought they just wanted me out of the way," said Sepia.

"I know, plus Mistress Calisto lacks certain social skills, like explaining things. Also Gan made sure no one said anything until we were in the tunnels," said Martha.

"We? It's only the two of us?" said Sepia.

"There will be more once we get to the end of the tunnel. Things have been happening outside and Gan felt it was important you not be alone," said Martha.

"Things, what things?" said Sepia.

"You've been declared a Black hunter. Worse, Overseer Marks has called you a Nightmare half-breed. You are to be executed on sight," said Martha. "They are saying you and Gan killed Overseer Peterson."

The words stunned Sepia into silence as they ran. Being called a Black hunter meant that every hunter would be after her. It was seen as a betrayal-- a stain on all hunters and what they stood for.

It was worse than being called a Nightmare, and he had called her that as well. *Martha, I hope you can fight. This party is about to get brutal,* thought Sepia.

SEVENTEEN

CHIMERA RODE HARD TO THE Hunter's keep. The mount he was on responded to his slightest touch, jumping over roots and large rocks. Behind him the Dreadwolves howled as several packs followed. Behind the wolves came the Brutes, which he would need to collapse the walls. *The witch dies tonight.* Approaching the bridge, he slowed and dismounted. He spoke to his mount in a whisper and tapped the side of its head. It turned and ran off.

"Hello, witch. I have come for the hunter," said Chimera as he turned around.

Calisto stood behind him with Ursa at her side. The bear snuffled at the stench.

"I see he likes me. Would you consider loaning him to me one day?"

Calisto clenched her jaw and took a deep breath, immune to the stench that surrounded the Nightmare Lord.

"There is no hunter here, you have come in vain," said Calisto.

Chimera pulled out a small knife and began to remove dirt from his fingernails. The bear took a step forward, protectively.

"Don't lie to me, witch. I can feel her in the keep. She hasn't aligned completely with her blade and that imbalance smells delicious." He tilted his head back and took a deep breath.

"You are mistaken and should leave now," said Calisto. She touched her hands together in what appeared to be prayer. She kept them together as she followed the Nightmare Lord with her eyes.

"I wanted to do this without bloodshed, witch, but you force my hand," said Chimera.

He put away his knife and put his hands in his pockets. Chimera took several steps forward over the bridge.

"I would hate to have to kill you," Calisto said as he drew closer. "Why do you want the hunter?"

"You know why. Centuries we have been kept in this gilded cage. Because they fear us, and they should. We are the rightful rulers of this world, not them," said Chimera.

His eyes began to flare several shades of green. The light cast his face in an unnatural shadow.

"And yet here we are, inside the cage," said Calisto.

"Not for long, witch. With the hunter's blood I can bring down the wards permanently and we will start with this city. We will continue until we have every city."

"What of the humans? Will you kill them all?" said Calisto.

Chimera made a face of mock shock. "Do you think I'm some kind of monster? Of course we won't kill them all. They will make excellent pets. Some will be converted, of course. I could always use more Brutes."

Chimera looked back as several Brutes crested the hills opposite the keep and made their way to him.

"What about the rest?"

"Why do you care? They trapped you the same way they trapped us. You should be joining me not standing in my way," said Chimera. "Besides, we should not worry about cattle. There are enough humans for all the Unholy to thrive."

"And you wonder why they fear you, and lock you away. They should have destroyed you when they had the chance," said Calisto.

"I seem to remember a hunter who felt the same way and said something similar right before I had her killed," said Chimera.

Calisto took a step back and spread her hands apart, materializing her sword.

"Now, witch, give me the hunter, and I will make sure her death is swift."

Calisto raised her sword and slammed it into the earth, point first. The ground around them shook and then settled.

"Was that it? A little earthquake?" said Chimera.

The Brutes had gathered by his side now. Several of them wore nervous expressions. Calisto stepped back even further when the tremors started again. Before her a chasm opened, swallowing half of the brutes, the other half started running away as the ground began to heave. A gulf opened separating Chimera and Calisto.

"You are prolonging the inevitable, witch. He turned to the Dreadwolves. "Go bring her to me—alive, if possible," Chimera said.

The pack of Dreadwolves took off to find the edge of the chasm.

Calisto drew closer to Ursa and whispered in her ear.

"This won't stop him for long. We need to be the distraction," said Calisto. She jumped on the back of Ursa as the bear ran deeper into the park. The wolves changed direction to follow them.

Chimera stood still for a moment looking into the night, his eyes shifting hue. Then he took a step into the chasm, and stepped on solid ground.

"An illusion," he said. He looked to the side to see the Brutes that had appeared to fall in the chasm. They lay on the ground in a state of paroxysm, bodies rigid.

"An illusion with very real effects," said Chimera. He stood over one of the Brutes and kicked it with no response.

"That was clever, witch, but pointless," said Chimera.

He walked toward the keep and stayed on the edge of the wards that kept it safe. Around him, the grass died and turned black.

"I'm going to assume the image of you running away was an illusion as well," he said.

Calisto stepped out in front of the keep. Ursa padded over to her side.

"You will not have her, Nightmare," said Calisto.

She took a defensive stance and faced Chimera. Ursa began a low growl as she hunched down, her muscles rippling.

"Nightmare, I am the nightmare? Have you seen what they do to us when we leave the park? I am the nightmare? They attack for no reason, without provocation, we are sport to them. Even our attackers are called hunters," said Chimera.

Ursa leapt into the air, aiming for Chimera, fangs and claws extended. Chimera made a slashing motion with his arm as the bear approached.

Ursa was caught mid leap and tossed to the side, crashing into a tree and splintering it with a sickening crunch. Ursa fell to the ground, lifeless.

"You should train your pets better," said Chimera.

"Damn you," she said through clenched teeth. She separated her hands and drew a sword of brilliant energy. Blue light coruscated around the blade, which glowed white.

Calisto ran toward Chimera, sword drawn. She lunged, her silver blade a slice of brilliance in the dark. Chimera stepped back, avoiding the point of the blade. She slashed horizontally to the left. He stepped into the arc of the blade and grabbed it with one hand, stopping it as his flesh burned.

"I don't want to kill you, witch, but I will if it gives me the hunter," he said. He shoved her back with a palm strike to her chest as he held on to the sword. The strike was so sudden she lost her grip and flew back several feet. He grabbed her sword by the hilt. The blade slowly began to turn black.

Calisto knelt on one leg and placed her hands together. As she separated her palms, another blade formed matching the first one.

"Is that an illusion? Let's find out."

He strode forward and slashed downward. Calisto parried the block but stumbled back. He slashed at her legs, forcing her to step back. Closing the distance faster than she could react, he punched her in the stomach. He slashed her thigh as she doubled over. Black ooze entered the wound from the blade.

"You must be quite strong, witch. That cut would have killed most. No matter, another one should finish you," said Chimera.

He advanced toward her as a pair of shots rang out dropping him to the ground. She looked down to see two bullet holes in the center of his forehead. She limped back to the keep as the main door opened. Gan ran out to help her in.

"That will only slow it down," she said.

"You're hurt. Let me take a look," said Gan.

Cade ran to close the keep door behind them. He looked outside and saw the still body of Chimera in the grass. He stayed near the arrow slit to see if the Nightmare moved.

"I can't imagine it's going to get up after two headshots," said Cade.

"You need to broaden your imagination, boy. It can and it will. Only way to end that one is to remove its head from its shoulders and burn the parts," said Gan.

"That's the only way?" said Cade

"And making sure the head doesn't fall anywhere near the body. Yes, that's the only way," said Gan. "You are looking at a genuine Nightmare Lord, emphasis on the Nightmare."

Calisto sat down on one of the benches in the foyer as Gan examined the wound. He saw the telltale signs of a widow's strike. The black network of lines was not spreading, remaining around the open wound. The wound was red and angry and looked infected.

"This looks bad, we need to get this treated now," said Gan. He started to stand up and she grabbed his hand.

"We don't have time. Did you send them to the tunnels?"

Gan nodded. "Martha and the Grey will get her somewhere safe. The Overseer has her blacklisted. How does it feel?" Gan said clearly worried about her wound.

"I've stopped the poison for now. We need to reverse the keep wards when it comes in," said Calisto.

"Reverse the wards?" Gan clenched his jaw and remained silent a moment. "You have to do that from inside the keep. It means you will be trapped inside with it," said Gan.

"I think it's strong enough to get out of the park. It wants Sepia for something inside the park. I think he will go after her. We need to stop him here, Gan," said Calisto.

Gan looked away, upset. She placed one hand on his cheek.

"There has to be another way, another way that we can stop him," said Cade. He looked outside the arrow slit and saw the body began to move.

"Shit, I can't believe I'm saying this, but it's not done. That thing is moving!"

Gan looked into Calisto's eyes. "Is there another way?"

She shook her head slowly, tears forming in her eyes at his pain.

"If I were stronger and had more time to plan, perhaps. As it stands, your shot only bought me enough time to prepare the wards for the inversion," she said. "It's time for you to leave, love. Please keep Sepia safe and prepare her. One day she will have to face this menace. I will make sure it's not today."

Gan stood slowly and turned to Cade.

"Pack up, we need to double time it out of here. Head to the other tunnel I showed you." Cade hesitated a moment and Gan grabbed him by the arm. "Let's go, gunman," said Gan. He knelt again and took Calisto's hand, holding it for a long moment then placed his hand on her face.

"I will see you again," he said.

"I know. Now go make sure Sepia and the rest are safe. I will keep the Nightmare here," said Calisto.

Gan and Cade headed for the tunnel on the opposite side of the keep followed by some of the house staff.

Calisto spoke to one of the remaining young girls from the keep and instructed her to make sure everyone left in the next few minutes with Gan. No one was to remain behind. She made her way to the warded room and looked around. *Even with the wards in place, she still managed to open the trapdoor. She is powerful. You would be proud Emiko,* thought Calisto.

She placed her hands together and this time when she separated them a latticework of blue light appeared before her. The latticework grew into a sphere that enveloped her and continued to expand outward, spreading over the entire keep. It flared a moment and then it faded into the stonework. Calisto waited.

****

The Nightmare Lord opened his eyes and stood. He turned and looked at the keep, his eyes shifting hues.

"That was a nice nap. They never learn…bullets, really? I will have to kill the witch later. First things first," said Chimera as he dusted off his clothes.

He walked towards the keep. As he drew closer, the ground began to smoke under his feet. He continued to get closer, his pace slowing feeling the strength of the wards. The door to the keep loomed before him. He placed both hands on the massive door, focused his energy, and pushed.

The door creaked and began to splinter. He pushed some more and the door shattered inward, wood and stone flying everywhere. Stepping through the threshold, the latticework flared for a brief second. He paid it no mind. Walking through the foyer, he followed the presence of the hunter until he arrived at a room that had its door covered in wards. He pushed open the door and looked. Inside this room, he felt the hunter. He peered in the room and saw a figure sitting on the bench furthest from the door. He stepped in, causing the latticework to flare a second time. Sensing something wrong he turned to exit the room and found he couldn't cross the threshold. He turned around, his eyes flaring green and casting sickly shadows along the walls.

"How are you still alive, witch? That wound should have killed you long ago," he said.

"I am not without my skills, creature," said Calisto.

"I promise you a swift death. Undo these wards," he said.

He took several steps towards her when he noticed the pool of blood at her feet.

"What have you done?" asked Chimera.

"I hope you like your new home. As homes go, it's not the worst. I have had some pleasant memories here. You will be cut off from the energy of the park and so each day you will grow weaker, until you cease to exist," said Calisto. She fell to the floor and sat down.

"You used a blood ward? Do you know what you have done?" Chimera said, rage filling his voice.

He stood still. The rage came off him in waves. His eyes shone a deep orange, bathing the room with bright light.

"I am aware of what I have done. My life is forfeit and now tied to the energy of this keep. You will remain here for a very long time, creature, as it slowly siphons your life-force," said Calisto.

She closed her eyes and her head slumped forward. Chimera strode over to her body and picked her up by the neck.

"It will not be that easy, witch. You may have trapped me, but I will not be alone."

He sent a jolt of black energy into her body and her eyes shot open.

"What have you done?" said Calisto.

"I too have my skills, witch. As long as I am a prisoner here, you will join me," he said.

"What? No! This cannot be," yelled Calisto. She looked down at her body. It was translucent.

She tried to break free from his grip and found it impossible.

He let go of her neck and she fell to the floor. He looked down at her as he spoke.

"It can and it will be. Time is irrelevant to me. You sought to escape me with death. As long as I exist, we are bound. You will haunt this place for as long as I do. My energy has merged with that of this place. You cannot escape me now. This keep is now your prison as well."

He stepped across the threshold, now free to travel throughout the keep.

"You will not need food or sleep. You are somewhat dead, after all. You have just prolonged the inevitable. I will escape this prison of yours and I will find the hunter and I will release my brethren, the Unholy. It's only a matter of time," said Chimera.

"You will never escape this place, creature. I am prepared for my fate and accept it willingly," said Calisto. The defiance in her voice rang throughout the room, challenging the Nightmare Lord.

"You dare?" He whipped his arm around, his face a visage of rage.

She stood still as he extended his arm at her. Black ooze washed over her, but left her untouched. He narrowed his eyes and looked at her, then turned around and walked away.

"It would appear being dead does have its benefits," said Calisto. She cried silent tears.

EIGHTEEN

SEPIA AND MARTHA RAN DOWN the tunnel to the very end. It had turns and bends but none of them were sharp. It kept leading them towards the west side of the park. Behind them they could hear the young men and women of the keep. Many had joined them along the way to the West Side exit. As they ran Sepia could see that the main tunnel had branches that would lead in different directions. These branches were smaller than the main tunnel.

Over time they no longer heard any running behind them.

"They must have split up," said Sepia.

"They have different instructions. In the case of an evacuation or in an emergency if they are being chased, they present multiple targets," said Martha.

"I wonder who taught them that," said Sepia.

"I did, now keep going." It was Gan.

Gan seemed to materialize from thin air. Sepia jumped, startled.

"By all that's holy, Gan, could you warn me when you're going to do something like that?" said Cade. "I didn't even see them ahead. I could have shot you."

"She should have sensed you," he said pointing at Sepia. "As for you shooting me that's not very likely. You're a piss poor shot. I think I'll take my chances," said Gan as he slung his rifle over his shoulder.

"Where's Calisto?" said Sepia.

Gan stopped for a moment and paused.

"Calisto isn't coming with us," said Gan.

"What do you mean she isn't coming? You told me there was a Nightmare Lord. You told me it was off the charts. I knew we should have stayed," said Sepia.

"If you had, you would probably be dead right now," said Gan. "She did what she felt she had to do to buy you and us time."

"You mean…?" said Sepia.

"Did she sacrifice her life for you? No, she sacrificed her life for all of us," said Gan.

He kept moving down the tunnel. The rest followed in silence. They followed the tunnel until they saw the exit up ahead.

"It's almost morning. We wait here until dawn and the hunters end their patrols," said Gan.

"How far is it to the safe house from here?" Cade said as he adjusted his rifle.

"This tunnel will let us out at 79th and Columbus. It's inside a parking garage so we should avoid the hunters at least initially," said Gan.

Cade began working on his weapon, checking it and making sure every part moved smoothly. Sepia sat alone in silence.

Cade looked over at Sepia and then turned to Gan, his voice lowered.

"Is the blacklist true?" said Cade. Gan nodded.

"If my source is correct, Overseer Marks not only blacklisted her but said she was half Nightmare."

"Shit, this is bad," said Cade.

"She is also implicated in the Peterson incident, as an accessory. He is trying to pin that one on me," said Gan.

"What the hell? Why you?" said Cade.

"We're convenient. He wants power and grabbed it. He needed a scapegoat and we were perfect. We were seen fleeing the scene by several witnesses. It was a good setup," said Gan.

Sepia had walked over quietly to where Gan and Cade were sitting.

"Whose sector are we in?" said Sepia.

"This is sector ten. Andrews' and Mc Daniels' sector," said Gan

Cade whistled low. "I've heard about those two. They are serious business."

"Yes, those two are a veteran hunter team, fifteen years. Our only saving grace is that the Overseer for this area is Wright. It may buy us a day or two," said Gan.

"Wasn't she a hunter?" said Sepia. Gan nodded.

"Rebecca was one of the best, easily a class two. No one thought she could make Overseer. She proved them wrong," said Gan. "She won't follow Marks's orders blindly. If I know her she'll attempt a capture, even with the blacklist on Sepia."

"Well, Andrews and McDaniels are good. I came up in gun school with Mac, good guy, great shot," said Cade. He put his rifle together and pulled back the slide.

"I'm not going to kill another hunter," said Sepia.

"No one is asking you to. Besides you still need training," said Gan. He looked at his watch. "Okay, it's time-- let's go."

They left the tunnel and entered the garage through a door marked Authorized Personnel. Gan opened another door and spoke to the parking attendant. They waited as the attendant brought their vehicle up.

"I wonder how many of those tunnels lead to places like this in the city," said Cade. "It would be good to know where they all lead."

"He knows, and there is a map at the Grey command that has all of that information and more," said Martha as she pointed at Gan.

The attendant brought up a black Suburban, and they all got in with Martha driving. Gan paid the attendant and they drove out of the garage.

"Is this an Order vehicle?" said Sepia.

"Yes, I had it stripped down to nothing and then reassembled. Why are you asking?" said Gan. Sepia pointed behind her to the vehicles following them. "Because of them," she said.

"Hell, we need to lose them, Martha," said Gan.

"Guys, can this thing take armor piercing rounds?" said Cade.

"That would make them too heavy. Small arms fire, yes, heavy calibers no, oh shit," said Sepia.

"What?" said Gan.

"There's a fifty cal. peeking out of the window on the passenger side, second truck back," said Cade.

"Martha, we do not want to get hit by that thing. No way can we stop that kind of firepower," said Sepia.

"I'm on it," said Martha as she cut the wheel a hard left and headed towards Broadway.

Martha began weaving in and out of traffic, putting as many obstacles as she could between them. Gan began making calls to set up interference. One truck managed to follow down the street. The second overshot the turn and continued on to the next street, making a left at the corner.

"Help is on the way," said Gan. They screeched onto Broadway and Martha turned on her lights, which notified local law enforcement this was Order business. The second vehicle made the turn and Sepia could see them gaining.

"We have trouble coming in fast on the right," said Sepia.

The next moment, a garbage truck that was idling on the street slammed into the second vehicle, sending them down a side street across Broadway toward the West Side Highway. The garbage truck blocked the street forcing the pursuers to back up. A second garbage truck prevented them from exiting the street.

"What was that?" said Sepia.

"That was help, but it won't last long. We need to get off the streets. I'm pretty certain those weren't Wright's men --not with a fifty caliber loaded for bear," said Gan.

"Where to, sir?" said Martha.

"Take us to the nearest subway. We need to get underground, away from peering eyes," said Gan.

****

It had been a week and no word. Marks initiated the blacklist on the second day, hoping to flush out Sepia. It was clear she wasn't on the streets. That left the park. *Why did Chimera go silent?*

"Sir?" It was Benson.

Marks snapped from his reverie. "Yes, what is it?"

"They evaded our men, and there is a call for you on line one."

"The incompetence of this organization never ceases to amaze. It's not like they have anywhere to go. Who is on line one?" said Marks.

Line one was reserved for the higher ranked officers of the Order. Marks hated line one.

"Overseer Wright, sir," said Benson as he left the office.

Marks took a deep breath. This would require tact.

"Hello Rebecca," said Marks. His tone was neutral and business like.

"Jonathan, explain to me why I have your men chasing a vehicle in my district? Does Regional know about this or is this one of your unsanctioned actions?"

Does she know about Peterson? How could she know? She can't possibly know. "Rebecca, I don't know what you are referring to. My men are simply working on evasive driving maneuvers," he lied.

"Marks, don't bullshit me. Pull your men out of my district now or I will allow my men to convince them to leave with extreme prejudice," warned Rebecca. She hung up the phone.

Marks picked up the phone. "Benson, get my men out of there, now."

"Yes, sir," said Benson.

Marks picked up the phone again. He hated the idea of delegating this, but had no choice at the moment. After a few seconds, a woman answered.

"Yes?" the woman said.

"The hunter is moving, but I can't touch her. I need you to bring her to me dead or alive --the payment is the same."

"Dead, then," said the woman.

"Make sure you aren't seen," said Marks.

Silence was his answer for several seconds. "The only way someone sees us, is if we want them to. It is usually the last thing they see," said the woman.

"I would expect nothing less. I will send you her last known position," said Marks and hung up. He disliked dealing with the Sisters. They were always a last resort, a heavy handed weapon, once unleashed impossible to retract. If the blacklist didn't eliminate Sepia, the Sisters would.

There was a knock on the door to his office.

"Come in," said Marks. A tall figure walked in dressed in a business suit. His features were average --forgettable with the exception of a small mark on the side of his neck. It was the mark of a chimera.

NINETEEN

"THE CLOSEST SUBWAY STATION is 86th Street sir," said Martha.

"That's close enough. Take us there, then take the truck and head back to Command. Make sure you aren't tailed," said Gan.

Martha pulled the SUV up to the corner of 86th and Broadway. They stepped out of the vehicle and Martha turned to Sepia. She lowered the window and extended her hand.

"It was an honor, Sepia. No matter what they say, you're solid in my book," said Martha. Sepia took her hand to shake it when the hairs on the back of her neck stood on end. She shifted to the left to look behind her, uneasy. When she turned she noticed the small hole in Martha's forehead. Martha slouched lifeless in the driver's seat.

"Gunman! Down Sepia!" said Cade. They rushed down the subway stairs.

"Goddammit, she was one of my best," said Gan through clenched teeth. Gan took out his phone. "Send a crew to 86th and Broadway. Grey agent down. Take her back to Command. Treat the vehicle as compromised, destroy it. There may be possible Sister involvement."

"What kind of ordnance was that, Gan? I've never seen a shot that didn't leave a bloody mess on the exit," said Cade. "Who are the Sisters?"

Gan walked to the end of the platform and headed down to the tracks with Sepia and Cade in tow.

"Every five years, one hundred hunters are recruited. They are usually from the best and the brightest. In many cases, like yours, Sepia, they are the daughters of current hunters who have come of age. Those are the ideal, but rare," said Gan.

"How many make it?" said Sepia. She remembered the difficulty of the qualification and training process.

"Maybe half of them, but most of the time it's only twenty or thirty. Some die during the training. I'm sure you remember losing some trainees when you went through hunter Training," said Gan

Sepia nodded. They had lost forty recruits her year, which was considered a bad one. Forty recruits had made it and the last twenty failed the training. She didn't know this was the norm.

"The recruits that fail are put into the Sisters Program. There they hone their skills and are put on a different track," said Gan.

They had walked quite a distance in the tunnel until Gan found the door he was looking for. He pushed it open and several young men dressed in gray camouflage approached him. They walked down a corridor heading toward a nexus of activity.

"What kind of track?" said Cade. He had an idea where this was heading.

"The ordnance you saw take down Martha is what we call drill ammo. It's a bullet and rifle pair. The rifle is designed with a special barrel that increases the revolution of the bullet to such a degree that when it hits the target, rather than just impact, it drills its way through," said Gan.

"Clean kills and minimal trajectory trace," said Cade.

"Exactly. The Sisters Program was officially discontinued by Regional several years ago. Unofficially it was kept up and running," said Gan.

"So these are assassins trained by the Order?" said Sepia. The anger was evident in her voice.

Gan turned to her. "I know you don't believe in killing. Not everyone shares that position. In fact the Sisters are one of the most efficient and ruthless organizations in the world. They will not hesitate to take you down, and lose no sleep over it."

"World class assassins are after us," whispered Cade. He rubbed his hand through his hair.

"Worse. These are assassins with most of the skills of a hunter, trained by the Order. They don't stop and they never fail to complete an objective. They would rather die than fail," said Gan.

A young man came running up to Gan handing him a piece of paper. Gan's faced paled.

"Are you certain about this?" said Gan.

"We ran the data three times, sir. Yes, we are sure," said the young man. His face was grim and a thin sheen of sweat covered his brow. Gan sat down hard at one of the desks in the control center.

"What is it, Gan?" said Sepia.

"Trouble we can't afford," said Gan.

He handed her the paper, and she read it twice-- unable to make the words have meaning. Cade took the paper from her stiff hands and read the document.

"By all that's holy," whispered Cade.

"How could this be?" said Sepia. "How is this even possible? Can we stop it?"

"I wish I had an answer for you. If there is one, there is only place it will be and that's in the Archives. This means we need to go Home before it's too late," said Gan.

Cade looked down at the paper again, unable to believe his eyes. If the breaches continued their present course, in one year all the wards around the park would fail, unleashing the Unholy into the world. Everything they fought for would be destroyed.

****

Marks looked at the figure as he sat down before the desk. The chimera tattoo shifted and changed with every movement.

"Your name is?" said Marks.

"Irrelevant, my purpose here however is not," said the man. "However, you can call me Onyx," said the man.

"Like the stone?" said Marks.

"Precisely, and I've come to deliver a message," said Onyx.

"How did the hunter escape the park? I sent her straight to you. This is ridiculous! I'm doing my part, but he isn't keeping up his end of our deal," said Marks.

Onyx sat still and waited for Marks to finish.

"Would you like me to relay your words to him?" said Onyx.

Marks paused and became subdued.

"My apologies, I am letting the situation get the best of me. Please deliver your message."

"My master has met with some, complications. It would greatly facilitate your mutual goals if you managed to debilitate the wards further," said Onyx.

"How am I supposed to do that? The knowledge of the wards has been lost for centuries," said Marks.

"You have a repository of knowledge here, an archive? I would start there," said Onyx.

"Wait, are you saying he needs help?" Marks's mind began to turn. There was an advantage to be had here.

"I think help is a strong word. The choice is yours after all. You can do as instructed or wait and do nothing," said Onyx.

Marks knew what the outcome would be if he chose to do nothing.

"I will find a way to weaken the wards," said Marks.

"I think that is the right choice," said Onyx.

Onyx stood to leave and paused. He picked off some of the lint from his suit. "Overseer, don't underestimate this hunter. She has powerful allies. Powerful enough to inconvenience my master. The measure of an enemy can be seen in who stands with them in times of adversity," said Onyx as he left the office.

****

"How are we going to get into Home? The place is a fortress," said Cade. They were in a conference room with blueprints spread out across the table.

"Two things help us. One, the place is huge, so getting in past certain areas shouldn't be too hard. Two, it's the last place they would expect us to be," said Gan.

"That doesn't sound easy," said Sepia." It doesn't help that I'm blacklisted."

"Home isn't the problem, it's the Archives," said Gan. He turned one of the pages over and began to trace a line.

"What's that?" said Sepia.

"This is an old, unused sewer line. It was shut down when this wing was erected because the foundation cut right into it."

Sepia looked down and traced the line with her finger. The line led from the Home main structure to deep within the park.

"This line goes into the park pretty deep," she said. She looked to see if there were any other options and found none.

Cade put his finger on the blueprints and followed another line out.

"How about this one? It leads out to a large flat area not too far from Home." Gan looked down at the blueprints and shook his head.

"That won't work. That flat area is now a lake," said Gan.

"I don't like it, Gan. This puts us in a bad situation if we get spotted in the park," said Sepia.

"I know, but we don't have a choice. That is the only way in and out."

"How many are we taking in with us?" said Cade.

"It's going to be us. A small team has a better chance with this," said Gan.

We have to approach from the park," said Cade.

"I'm not looking forward to going in there again," said Sepia. Gan grew quiet and she realized he was thinking of Calisto.

"I'm sorry I didn't mean to," she said.

"I know and it's okay. I'm going to call in some favors and see if we can get dropped in," said Gan.

Sepia looked at Cade. "Dropped in, into the park?" she said.

"It's the safest way in," said Gan.

"This sounds crazy. Hell, if I'm going to die, this would be the way to go," said Cade.

He had a wide grin on his face as he left the conference room headed for the armory. Sepia began to look at the blueprints again and taking notes.

"What are you doing?" said Gan. He peered over her shoulder at the notes.

"Making sure I know these tunnels. Last thing I want is to get lost while some Nightmare is chasing me from the park."

"Make sure Cade knows them too," said Gan.

"How soon are we leaving?" asked Sepia.

"You have a few hours still. We need to get out there by nightfall. Try and get some rest before we leave," said Gan.

"Because doing this during the day would be too safe?"

"Because doing this during the day would get us killed, if the Sisters are looking for us."

"You never said how we were getting into the Archives --what is the security down there?"

"Leave that to me, I'll get us in. You'll get us out," said Gan.

****

Marks called in Benson to his office.

"How much of the Archives are on the network?" said Marks.

"All of it, sir," said Benson. Marks sighed with relief. *This is going to be easier than I thought.*

"I need information on the wards, how they function and why," said Marks.

"That information is going to be a little harder to get, sir."

"You just told me all of the Archives are on the network."

"I know, but that only applies to the last hundred years. The wards are several hundred years old." *I should have known that. Ignorance is weakness. I must not appear weak,* thought Marks.

"Is there a way to access the information remotely?" said Marks.

"No, that information is sealed away and pretty old. To access that will require going down into the Archives," said Benson.

Marks cursed under his breath.

"How soon can I go there?" said Marks.

"The Archive locks are on timers. No one can open them before they are set to open and I mean no one. The door down there makes a bank vault look like a screen door," said Benson.

"When are they set to open Benson?" His ignorance of this matter made him feel off balance.

"They are set to open every night, sir, at midnight, about two hours from now."

137

"Is there any special clearance required, or do I have to call Regional?" *I really hope that isn't necessary.*

"Only to access the most dangerous places do you need Regional to be informed, then they send one of their people if the request is made. We won't need that for the Antiquities section. Besides, you're an Overseer, sir. You can go there anytime you like," said Benson.

"How do you know all of this, Benson? This isn't in the Order agent training," said Marks.

"I try to learn everything about the Order, and it was also my post before I was promoted to field work, sir," said Benson. *This one has ambition. I will have to keep my eye on him and keep him close,* thought Marks.

"Can we go down earlier?" It wouldn't be nightfall for several hours yet, but he wanted to get this information as soon as possible.

"Yes, sir, we can head down we just can't enter the Archive proper until midnight," said Benson.

"Let's head down, then. I need to get some information on the wards and why they are failing. We need to keep our city safe and those wards are our first line of defense," said Marks.

They made their way to an elevator that was reserved for the use of the Overseer and his second in command. It had small benches affixed to the sides to provide seating. Marks put his hand on the panel that was devoid of buttons and the elevator doors closed with a rush of air. After a few seconds the elevator began its descent.

"I have never had a need to travel to the Archives. You worked there, so you would know this. How far down are we headed?" said Marks.

138

"The Archives are located roughly five hundred feet below the surface, sir."

"Why so deep? The subways aren't even that deep," said Marks. Being that far below ground made Marks uncomfortable. "It feels like entering a tomb."

"Yes, sir. It was placed that deep as a security measure. Some of the items in the Archive have been deemed extremely volatile," said Benson.

"Which items?" said Marks.

"I'm not at liberty to say, sir. I was never cleared for that area of the Archives," said Benson.

The whirr of the air conditioner kicked in as they kept descending. Even with it going on the highest setting, the elevator was getting warm.

"It gets hot down there, sir. You may want to take off the tie and jacket," said Benson.

Marks kept his jacket on but loosened his tie. He could feel the sweat form under his arms and running in rivulets down his back.

"How long does this ride take?" said Marks as he took off his tie and unbuttoned the top shirt buttons. He didn't know if it was the heat or being in such a small elevator. It felt confining.

"It's because of the pressure, sir. As the elevator goes down its equalizing the pressure so we can adjust to the depth," said Benson.

"That is not a time, Benson. I asked how long?" said Marks.

"About an hour and a half sir," said Benson. He could see the discomfort of the Overseer wash across his face.

"It would seem we have a long ride before us then," said Marks. He sat down on one of the benches and took some calming breaths. *I must not show weakness.*

TWENTY

SEPIA AND CADE WERE IN the conference room going over the plans one last time when Gan entered.

"Let's go our ride is up top," said Gan.

"What do you mean up top? If we hit street level we are pretty much done," said Cade.

"I didn't say anything about street level, now let's go," said Gan. He headed down a corridor. At the end of the corridor was a set of doors that were done in an ornate art deco style.

"What are we under?" said Sepia.

Gan pressed his hand to the panel beside the doors and they opened. It was an elevator.

"We are now below the San Remo. This elevator will take us to the top of the South Tower, where our ride will pick us up," said Gan. He entered the elevator, waited for Sepia and Cade and pressed his hand on a panel closing the doors. They ascended to the top several minutes later. The doors opened on a penthouse balcony with a stunning view of Manhattan.

Over the Park Sepia could see the air shimmer with energy. The wards completely enveloped the park creating a large dome-like roof.

"How is the Grey connected to the architecture of the city? It seems that you know a lot about the city that most don't, not to mention access to things like this," Sepia said as she pointed to the elevator.

"One of the assistant architects of this building was in the Order. When construction began in 1929, the Order made sure they had access to it," said Gan.

"How old exactly is the Order?" said Cade.

"Understand that the Order predates this city. Most of the founders were hunters who fought the Unholy not just here but all over the world," said Gan.

"Why contain them in the park, couldn't we just drive them out?" said Sepia.

"The Unholy first appeared in the park. It seems they originate there. The park itself goes back to the 1800s. That is when the original treaty was created with the Unholy giving them that land. Calvert Vaux was one of the first Overseers of the Order," said Gan.

"So they conceded to giving them that land? Instead of what?" asked Sepia.

"By that time the war had been raging for decades. Hunters, men, and women back then were dying every day. The Unholy were taking losses too, just not nearly as much as we were. We were winning the battles, but losing the war. The Unholy didn't know that due to their command structure. We bluffed them into a truce," said Gan.

"And now they are calling our bluff," said Sepia.

"You could say that, yes," said Gan.

They could hear the sound of a helicopter approaching them.

"That sounds like a UH-60, a Black Hawk." Cade peered into the night using his night vision goggles. "It looks a little small, though," said Cade.

"That's our ride," said Gan. It made one pass and then circled around the tower. Once the helicopter drew close to the building, it grew silent.

"You know your birds. It's a Black Hawk design but modified by the Order for urban warfare," said Gan.

"The stealth mode was nice touch," said Cade.

The helicopter drew close and hovered over the balcony. It was a black silhouette against the sky. The co-pilot waved his arm in a circular motion.

"That's our cue. Get on," said Gan. They boarded the helicopter and shut the cargo door. Inside, the helicopter was quiet with amber night running lights bathing the cockpit in their glow.

"Welcome aboard, sir. Is this all of you?" said the pilot.

"Yes, let's get over the park, we need to execute a LALO right over this location," said Gan. He pointed to a location on the map he held. The pilot looked at the location and then looked up at Gan.

"Are you sure, sir? That is going to be dicey," said the pilot.

"What's your name pilot?" said Gan.

"People call me Bear, sir." The name fits. Bear was a large man that filled up his side of the helicopter.

"Okay, Bear, this isn't my first jump in the pool. You keep the bird moving, get us over this location and I will take care of the rest," said Gan.

"The EMP activity is strong in that area. We couldn't stop if we wanted to. We won't be able to extract you, sir. This is one way, so are you sure?" Bear said as he looked at the map.

"I'm sure. That is our drop zone. How soon before we get there?" said Gan.

The pilot looked at the map again as he checked his watch.

"ETA is ten minutes, sir," said Bear.

"Sounds good. Let me know when we are one minute out," said Gan.

"Yes, sir," said Bear. He moved back into his seat and took over the controls. Putting on his headset he told the co-pilot where they were headed. The co-pilot shook his head as he looked back at the trio, his face impassive, and adjusted his instruments.

"Cade and I will use low opening chutes, you will just drop in. You should be able to recover fairly quickly from the jump," said Gan.

Sepia nodded and looked at the map.

"We're going to be exposed when we land," said Sepia.

"Yes, that's the edge of the Great Lawn. See that manhole cover? That's our entrance. It works on an old tumbler system so I'm going to need a few minutes to open it. Those few minutes means we may have company," said Gan.

"Why not just blow it?" said Cade.

"Why don't I just send out invitations to all the Unholy that we are coming too?" Gan said.

Cade grunted. He didn't like the idea of just standing around while Gan opened a door. It meant sitting there, waiting. *Might as well paint red circles on our backs,* he thought.

"One minute, sir," said Bear.

Gan and Cade adjusted their chutes while Sepia made sure her blade was tight in its scabbard. The last thing she needed was losing her blade in the middle of the park.

"Remember the coms will only work on burst transmissions in the park. Factor in the lag time," said Gan.

"It's time to go, sir!" said Bear. The co-pilot had opened the side door and Sepia could see the ground racing beneath them. Cade jumped out followed by Gan. She could see the instrument panel light up with warnings in every section. The EMP effect of the park was getting through the shielding.

"Thank you," said Sepia as she headed out of the helicopter. The co-pilot nodded and then she was airborne. Sepia loved jumps. The first few seconds felt like freedom. The air rushed around and it felt like flight. Seconds later gravity kicks in and the realization hits: This isn't flying --it's falling, and fast.

She could see the chutes as they made their way to the landing zone. She would get there before them. She tucked her arms and angled her body as she saw the great lawn. She braced her body for the impact as she extended her arms. She hit the ground and executed several rolls to dissipate the energy of the fall. From the rolls she began to run. Her ink flared in her arms and legs, mitigating any damage the fall had done. She drew her blade as she heard the footfalls behind her.

"We have company," she said into her com.

"We're almost down. Keep them away from the LZ," said Gan.

She ran parallel to the landing zone hoping to draw off whatever was following her. As she veered off she heard the footfalls turning as they continued following her.

"Shit-- it's me they're after," said Sepia. "Sounds like a group of Unholy coming our way."

"You're going to have to keep them busy Sepia. Intercept and engage," said Gan.

Sepia changed her direction and ran toward the footsteps. Whatever creatures made that noise they were not being subtle. It seemed like a large group and it was moving fast. Blade in hand, she managed to get a glimpse of it. It wasn't a group, it was one large creature.

"Gan, we have trouble. What is larger than a Brute and moves just as fast as a Nightmare?"

"Does it look like a Brute but just extra-large?" said Gan.

"This thing left extra-large several sizes ago. It makes Brutes look practically tiny," said Sepia. She led the large creature away from the others, cutting a path through the park.

"How can something so large be so fast?" Sepia said to herself.

"Sepia, bring it here. Don't attempt to stop it alone-- that thing is a behemoth. Do not engage it alone," said Gan.

"You may as well tell her to attack it. She can't resist a challenge like that," said Cade. Gan and Cade had landed near the entrance to the tunnel. Cade began looking for higher ground while Gan started working on the door.

"I got them. They just ran over that outcropping of boulders. By all that's holy, what the hell is that?" said Cade.

He perched himself in a tree and was looking through his scope.

"That thing is huge. Even with its size, I don't think I can hit it from here, they're moving around too much," said Cade.

"It wouldn't do much good even if you could. I can't believe they would let a behemoth out," said Gan.

Sepia had gotten its attention and it was angry.

"Does this thing have any weaknesses?" said Sepia.

"Yes, but you're not going to like it."

"The head again, right? What is it with Nightmares and decapitations?" said Sepia.

"It makes them very hard to eliminate. Behemoths are Brutes that were subjected to further transformation. Nothing hurts them or stops them except removing their heads. They are as difficult as any other Nightmare," said Gan. "Just make sure it doesn't hit you. Your ink won't be able to deal with that much damage at once and will shut you down," said Gan.

Sepia turned to face the creature. It stood ten feet tall. Its hands were larger than her head. Its body looked like a boulder come to life—sharp angles and lines. If it sat still she would have mistaken it for one. She looked closely at the eyes. She expected to see a mindless monster, but what she saw was intelligence.

The behemoth stopped and looked at her.

"I have its attention, now what?" she said.

"Don't let it come near you. You're going to have to lose it in the park then make your way back to us. You have five minutes once I get the door open," said Gan.

"Oh, that's it? Just lose it in the park that is crawling with the Unholy and head back? Should be a cakewalk," she said.

Sepia drew closer to the behemoth. Realizing shooting it wouldn't do much she opted for her blade. As she got closer the behemoth swung a massive arm around. She ducked under the arm only to face the kick that was coming at her. It was too late to dodge. She managed to get her sword up in time and deflected the kick. The force of the impact sent her flying.

"Sepia! That thing just launched her!" said Cade.

"Sepia, are you okay?" said Gan.

"I'm okay," she groaned. "I had my sword up."

She looked around and saw the kick had sent her flying back about a hundred feet. She could see where her blade had cut a trench in the ground. *Good thing I held on to this,* she thought as she looked at her sword. She swore that kick broke it, but the sword remained intact. The behemoth was making its way towards her.

"Tell me you have that door open," said Sepia.

"Thirty seconds and we're in. They must have expected something to unleash a behemoth. It's just odd that it would come toward us, --well, you. Wait a minute, Sepia. Your blade... Did you have it out during the drop?" said Gan.

"I took it out as soon as I landed," said Sepia. She was running fast now making a large circle to end up back where the others were.

"It must have something to do with your heightened alignment," said Gan.

"My what?" she said.

"On occasion with the named blades, when the hunter aligns with it there is a nasty side effect."

"I know I'm not going to like this," she said.

"The blade acts as a beacon. It attracts the Unholy. The higher the hunter's class the worse the Threat level of the Unholy. That would explain a few things, actually."

"And you didn't think this was relevant information before now, before we were in the middle of the park?" said Sepia.

"Gan, she's coming around and that moving boulder is getting close," said Cade.

"Door is open, Sepia. It won't fit in the entrance, which doesn't mean it won't try. Head right in and don't stop," said Gan.

Cade had gone inside the tunnel and set up a firing position. Gan waited outside for Sepia.

Cade set his scope and looked into the night. As soon as he saw Sepia he started firing past her.

The rifle made quiet whispers in the night sending bullets with explosive rounds towards the behemoth. Sepia had placed her blade in its scabbard, but the behemoth had zeroed in on her. She saw the entrance and ran for it. Gan had stepped out behind Sepia and directly in front of the charging behemoth. His hands glowed a deep red.

"What are you doing?" Sepia said as she ran past him.

"Buying us some time."

Assuming a low stance he waited until the behemoth was close. Executing a double palm strike under the behemoth, he pushed up with his legs and unbalanced the creature. The behemoth-- momentarily in the air looked around for Sepia before it was sent flying several feet away from the entrance.

Gan jogged over to the entrance, his hands looked like fresh ingots.

"What the hell, old man? How did you do that?" said Cade.

"Remember, always push with the legs."

"Let's get this door closed before we attract more attention." Gan began the sequence that sealed the door.

"You," he said pointing at Sepia, "make sure that blade stays in its scabbard unless we have no choice."

Sepia nodded and tightened the straps on her blade, which would prevent it from leaving the scabbard.

"We have to be careful not to trip any of the alarms in the tunnel or this will become a bad night indeed," said Gan.

The dimly lit tunnel featured old stone work dating back at least a hundred years. A small stream ran through the center. The ceiling was arched and the group could stand abreast of each other as they walked down. Behind them the muffled pounding of the behemoth could be heard. Dust from the ceiling jarred loose with each blow.

"Can it get through that door?" asked Cade.

"Even if it could it couldn't follow us. I would be more concerned with the things that are in here," said Gan.

"In here? What is in here, old man?" said Cade.

"Things to keep beasts like that out," said Gan.

"How are we going to get past these traps or deterrents, whatever you want to call them?" said Sepia.

"The best way to get past these traps, especially since we don't know what kind or where they are, is to trip them," said Gan.

"Say that again?" said Cade.

"We go straight ahead to the Archives and we deal with whatever we encounter," said Gan.

"I like that approach. Let's go," said Sepia.

"You would. Heading into a death pit and she likes that approach," grumbled Cade.

Gan took point and led the group. "Walk directly in the center of the tunnel. Don't touch the walls or anything else for that matter," said Gan.

The behemoth's pounding grew muffled as they made their way down the tunnel.

"One other thing, the actual Archive door won't be open until midnight. This tunnel will lead us to an atrium, where if we're lucky it will be empty," said Gan.

"That will be soon. What happens if we aren't lucky?" said Sepia.

"We can wait inside the tunnel until then. If we're unlucky there will be an atrium full of Order agents waiting for us," said Gan.

They made their way to the other end without incident.

"Is it possible there weren't any traps?" asked Sepia.

"That's unlikely considering where this tunnel goes and where it originates. Age is more likely a factor. This tunnel is old and unused, which means the precautions set in place were not needed since the tunnel itself was no longer used," said Gan.

"I for one am glad there weren't any. It's not like we don't have enough to deal with," said Cade.

Gan began working on the locking mechanism. It was more complex than the exterior lock, acting like a second line of defense.

"This may take a while. This lock is different from the one in the park. It's more recent and has more technology involved."

He took off his pack and began to remove some tools.

"That would make sense. This far away from the park, there is no need to worry about the EMP influence. What I don't understand is why they would bother to put a new lock on an unused tunnel…unless," said Sepia.

"Unless it's not unused," said Cade. "This just went from bad to horrible."

"You have no idea, gunman," said a voice behind them.

TWENTY-ONE

B Y THE END OF THE elevator ride, Marks had regained his composure. *I'm going to have to deal with Benson at some point.* The elevator doors opened to reveal a large waiting area. Several doors lined the walls. Most of them were bricked over.

"Is this place the Archives?" said Marks.

"Yes and no, sir. The Archives proper are behind that door."

Benson pointed to a large vault like door on the far end of the room. He made sure they avoided the door. Around it, wards fluctuated in color going from red to green to black.

"This area is what, then?"

"This is the Archive waiting area. There were times when the Order entertained foreign guests. This is where they would wait until the opening of the Archives," said Benson.

Marks looked around and noticed that the space looked very much like a fancy hotel lobby. He made his way over to the paintings on the walls. Each painting depicted a scene of battle from some point in history.

"Why battle scenes? Couldn't they have put something a bit more tranquil?" Marks said as he went from scene to scene.

"The reasoning I am told is that man in the midst of battle and wars unleashes great creativity and great destruction in equal measure. This symbolizes the items in the Archives," said Benson.

Marks made his way from painting to painting recognizing the scenes from some and having to read the plaques of others. Each painting was large, fitting in with the scale of the Archives.

"The access to the ward section…Will it be available to me when the door opens?" said Marks.

"Yes, sir, in a few minutes the timed lock will shift and the door will be accessible," said Benson.

"Is that what the wards are for, then?" said Marks.

He looked at the glowing wards and noticed Benson did not approach the door.

"Yes, sir. At the right time the wards become inactive making it possible to open the door. If you were to approach now well, it's not pretty," said Benson.

I can't get rid of him yet, but once he shows me what I need, I can dispose of him, thought Marks.

Marks shifted his jacket and felt familiar weight of his gun resting against his side.

"How often does someone come down here, Benson?"

"This area is visited daily to make sure there is regular upkeep. Certain parts of the Archives are also maintained on a regular basis. We are going to the Antiquities section. That area doesn't get much attention because it needs a higher level of clearance," said Benson.

"What level of clearance?"

"You need a second to the Overseer or higher. They also have surveillance in Antiquities to monitor the activity."

"What kind of surveillance?" *His disposal will evidently have to wait.*

"They're state of the art, sir. The cameras are set to see across every spectrum of light and even see in ways we wouldn't understand. At least that's what they told me when I was down here," said Benson.

On one side Marks could see a set of lights that were lit. One in particular was blinking rapidly.

"What are those lights?" said Marks.

"Those are tripwire lights. They are activated by movement in the unused section of tunnels below us."

"Does that happen often, those lights going off?

"All the time. Most of the lights go off when a rat or anything like that crosses into the old sewers," said Benson. He pointed at the old doors in the sealed stonework lining the doorways. Those lead to the old sewers but they were sealed long ago.

"The Archives are secure from this end so we don't pay any attention to them," said Benson.

Marks looked concerned. His instincts were telling him that it was no rat in those tunnels. *It's just nerves. Riding in that elevator set you on edge.*

"Has anyone ever gotten into the Archives this way?"

"It has never happened, sir. No one is crazy enough to approach from the park side."

Marks looked around at some of the doors set in the stonework. They all looked old except one, which looked recent.

"Why does that door have new locks?" said Marks.

The next few words were drowned out by crashing stones and debris that rushed into the waiting area. Marks and Benson ran to the opposite side as a body was flung into the room. It was Sepia.

Gan and Cade ran into the waiting area as the air in the room began to be siphoned out.

"What is that?" said Benson.

"Get down!" exclaimed Sepia as she leapt towards the entrance.

"That thing is a siroc. It will suck out all the air," said Cade.

"It must have followed us in, attracted to her blade," said Gan.

"I can't get a shot in, not with all that turbulence around it. He could probably just redirect and shoot one of us," said Cade.

"Sepia, you can't use the direct approach. It will just be deflected. You have to fight it in the tunnel. If you give it a wide open area we are done," said Gan.

"Got it, up close and personal it is," said Sepia.

She jumped into the tunnel and threw herself to the ground. A blast of compressed air missed her by inches and punched a hole in one of the side walls.

"You're fast for a human." It was a whisper but it carried throughout the tunnel. The Nightmare was dressed in tattered rags that whipped about its body with the winds it created. Its face was covered and only its eyes were visible. It reminded Sepia of a mummy. Except this mummy was pissed and managed to control air.

"Why don't I get easy Nightmares?" Sepia said as she dodged blast after blast in an effort to get closer to the Nightmare.

"I would really like a Nightmare of pillows or something like that," she said. A column of air hit her in the shoulder and slammed her into the wall of the tunnel.

"Shut up and focus, Sepia," said Gan.

"Why isn't it coming in farther?" said Cade

Gan looked around and then noticed the wards on the floor and the walls around the entrance to the Archives. The pulsing colors had changed to a deep blue.

"It must be the wards. "Sepia, those wards are going to come down soon, and then it will try and get in. If you're going to do something, it'd better be quick," said Gan.

"I am working on it," she said. Her ink had flared to handle the damage, the pain, she felt. She advanced on the Nightmare as it tried to hit her with blasts of air. The Nightmare drew closer and Sepia drew her blade. The Nightmare focused on her with intensity.

"Great--the blade makes things worse. Are you kidding me?"

Marks and Benson had found a hiding spot near the door to the Archives, on the other side of the waiting area.

"We need to get some more people down here now," said Marks.

"The elevator won't function if there is a breach. It's a failsafe. It means we are here alone with them," said Benson.

"That is what I call bad planning. Where do you think they will direct their attention once they are done with that thing?" said Marks.

It suddenly dawned on Benson.

"Oh, this is not good. There is another way up, but it's through the Archives, which are still closed," said Benson.

"For now we stay hidden. Once those wards come down we enter the Archives and keep them outside," said Marks.

Gan and Cade made their way back to the tunnel. Cade didn't risk a shot for fear of hitting Sepia. He pulled out his knife. Gan extended his hands and they began to smolder.

"Let's go, boy, she is going to need help," said Gan as he entered the tunnel. They could see Sepia getting closer to the siroc.

"I have an idea. I can use the flow of air to go past it and then come back," said Sepia.

"You're going to do what? That sounds like a recipe to get smashed against the wall, Blue," said Cade.

"It can work but you have to time it, Sepia. If you miss, Cade is right you will hit the wall at terminal velocity. We'll keep it away from the exit on this side," said Gan.

"You! You are the one who brought me here," said the siroc. It almost seemed as if the Nightmare were speaking to the blade and not to Sepia.

Sepia crouched down low and prepared to jump.

In the waiting area the wards flared blue and disappeared.

"Sir, the wards!" exclaimed Benson. He pointed to designs on the floor and walls around the Archive entrance as they slowly disappeared. The siroc sensed it as well and began to increase the force of the winds.

"Sepia, now would be a good time to do something!" said Gan. He and Cade were barely holding their ground as the wind increased in velocity.

"The wards must have dropped. It's getting stronger," said Cade.

Sepia jumped toward the Nightmare. The turbulence around it forced her to one of the edges and deflected her approach. She kept going past it and then stopped mid-air. For a split second, she was motionless in the middle of the tunnel and then her momentum reversed and she shot back toward the Nightmare.

Using her sword, she jammed it against the wall using it for leverage. Changing her trajectory she was no longer going around the Nightmare but straight for it. *This is not one of my best ideas,* she thought as she headed right at it.

"I don't think she's going to make it Gan," said Cade. They were both pressed against the wall, the force of the winds held them in place.

Bringing her knees into her chest, she curled into a ball and her velocity increased. At the last second, she straightened out and was buffeted to the right of the Nightmare. She extended her blade and removed the Nightmare's head as she fell to the ground and slid across the floor on her stomach. Water and dirt splashed into her face. The body of the Nightmare fell to the ground, reverting to dust.

"I don't ever want to do something like that again," she said.

They made their way slowly out of the tunnel and looked around. Gan noticed it first. The wards were back in place.

****

Marks and Benson were inside the Archives. It looked like a large storage facility with shelving as far as the eye could see.

"How large are the Archives?" said Marks.

"It's pretty immense, sir. There are maps but they only cover the central areas not the edges."

The sheer scope of the space impressed him. *This must have taken decades to build.* He looked around, taking in the entire view.

"No one knows for sure. It hasn't been measured recently. We don't have that kind of manpower," said Benson. Marks waved away Benson's answer.

"Never mind. Are you certain the wards are back in place? I don't want those three following us in."

"Yes, sir, the wards are back in place due to the breach. In case of a breach only an Overseer or higher can open the Archives. The wards come on automatically after the door closes," said Benson.

"Can anyone else open the Archives?" said Marks.

He wanted to make sure they were trapped. The only way out was through the tunnel that led to the park. *That's not an option I would choose.*

"That can only happen if they have the clearance equal to yours or higher. Only Miss. Wright has that kind of clearance, or someone from Regional."

"Good, that means they won't be going anywhere soon. Let's go to the Antiquities section-- I want to get the information I need and deal with the intruders as soon as possible," said Marks.

Benson led him through several sections. After a few minutes they all looked the same to Marks.

"How do you know where you're going? This place is like a maze. Every aisle looks the same," said Marks.

"When you get a position in the Archives, part of the training is learning the layout. Wouldn't make sense to have agents getting lost in a place this big," said Benson.

"You're trained not to get lost? How is this training done?"

"There are markers and small indicators on the floor at the end of each of the aisles."

Now that Benson pointed them out Marks could see the small plaques embedded into the floor at the end of each aisle. Marks crouched and looked closer. He brushed off a layer of dust and saw that it contained symbols and arrows.

"You can decipher this?" said Marks.

"We learn to read them. They let you know where you are in the Archives and how far from the next hub. Hubs are communication centers. In every hub there are a small number of agents. Hubs are also where you will find Archivists," said Benson.

"I see, so how far to the Antiquities section?" said Marks. Benson stood at the corner and read the small bronze plaque.

"It says there is a Hub fifty aisles over that way. We can ask there. I've never been to the Antiquities section but the Archivists there can point us in the right direction." They began walking towards the Hub.

****

"How are the wards back up? I thought they were on a timer?" said Cade.

"They are, now shut up and let me think," said Gan.

Cade moved off to one side muttering about suicide missions and how dying in a tomb was not his idea of fun.

"Sepia, when you first entered this area was it empty? I want you to think hard now," said Gan.

"I don't remember anyone. I came in kind of hard and then focused on the Nightmare.

"Replay the moment. Take a deep breath, hold it, and go over the events in your mind," said Gan.

"Gan, this isn't the time for…" began Cade. Gan held up his hand and shook his head.

"This is important. We need to know. If there was someone in here I have to do something that will bring the force of Home down on us. I'd rather not do that if I can help it."

"What do you mean the force of Home? The whole point of this exercise was to get in undetected. Not alert every agent in the building."

"Well, it's a little late for that. That Nightmare put a wrench in that plan when it destroyed the wall."

Cade threw up his hands, exasperated. "So if there was someone in here what will you have to do?"

"It will mean bypassing wards and using a clearance I didn't want to use, at least not yet," said Gan. "Let's hope it doesn't come to that."

Sepia sat in lotus position, calmed her breath and closed her eyes. Replaying the moment in her mind she felt the initial blast of air the Nightmare used to destroy the wall and send her flying through it. She saw herself tumble into the waiting area and over near the Archives door was someone, hiding.

"Shit, there was someone," she said as she opened her eyes and stood. She walked over to the place Marks and Benson used while she was fighting the Nightmare.

"Someone was crouched down here. I only remember one person but it could have been more," she said.

Gan turned and faced the Archives door. Careful to avoid the wards he began examining the wall beside the door.

"What are we looking for?" said Cade.

"There is a panel alongside here somewhere. I need to find that it."

****

Benson made a right turn fifty aisles later and led them into a large open area. Several counters were covered in computers. The Hub was deserted.

"That's strange. Usually the hubs are manned at all hours. It could be they have cut back," said Benson.

"Can we use one of the terminals?" said Marks.

"Sure, I still have my clearance. I can get us the information we need," said Benson.

He pulled up a stool and began typing at one of the terminals.

"Here we go. The Antiquities section is four aisles over and three aisles down," said Benson.

Marks looked over in the direction Benson indicated and could see nothing that would point to the Antiquities section.

"Are you certain? It doesn't look much different over there," said Marks.

"Yes, sir, they wouldn't move a section like Antiquities. Besides, most of it is under us in another level. The entrance is what this is pointing to."

"Under us," said Marks.

Benson turned the computer screen so Marks could see the map of the Archives with a grid overlaid on it. A large red arrow pointed to the location Benson had requested.

Marks saw the grid and realized that the level beneath was as extensive as the one he was currently on.

"How many levels are there?" Marks asked. His voice was a whisper as he thought of the implications of several levels.

"As far as I know there are only two levels. Some of the Archive rats --that's what we were called when I worked down here -- think there is another level beneath the Antiquities, but no one has found it."

"Let's go, we don't have all night," said Marks. Besides the information on collapsing the wards, he needed to find information on something else that would have to wait until he could disable the cameras and come down here alone.

Benson let Marks go ahead and stood back a few feet when they found the stairway to the Antiquities Section. Marks grabbed the door handle. After a few moments the door released and stale air greeted them.

"No security panel?" Marks wondered aloud. He looked for a place to press to open the door.

Benson pointed up to a small orb above the doorway.

"That's a biometric reader. It does face, iris, and retinal recognition. When you hold the handle it reads your DNA," said Benson.

"So, if I didn't have clearance?" said Marks.

"You would be a pile of ash, sir," said Benson.

It is a test of sorts. He wants to see if I have been telling the truth. Benson is more complex than I gave him credit for.

"Don't worry sir, you passed. I mean, the door recognized you. Let's go get that information. Then I can show you the other exit," said Benson.

"Do you know where the information on the wards is?" said Marks.

"I've never been in this area, but according to the terminal it should be right over...here."

Benson led them to an area of shelves covered in books. One book in particular stood out. The book was plain and had no title. It was about the size of a paperback and thin. On its cover were a series of designs that looked like the wards used in the park and in the Archives themselves. The other distinguishing feature was the absence of dust.

"That's odd. This book has been sitting here probably as long as the rest of these and yet, look-- no dust," said Benson as he made to grab the book. Marks grabbed his hand before he was able to touch the book.

"Why not take a precaution first? If it's a book on wards it stands to reason that the book itself may be protected," said Marks.

Marks removed a pen from his pocket and placed it near the book. Nothing happened. When he moved the pen to touch the book, the pen disintegrated in his hands.

"Well, that complicates things," said Marks. "Benson, go back to the hub and see if we need some kind of device or item to handle this book."

"Sounds like a good idea, sir. I'll be right back."

Marks looked around at the other books on the shelf. Nothing stood out as relevant. *It can be anything,* thought Marks. Benson came back moments later with what appeared to be a large towel. The cloth was covered in designs that mirrored the ones on the book.

"It says to drape the covering on the book, but be careful not to let the book touch anything except for the covering," said Benson. He handed the cloth to Marks. Marks looked at the cloth closely and saw nothing out of the ordinary, except when he shook it. The air around the cloth shimmered as if disturbed by heat. He placed the cloth on the book, covering it. He pulled out another pen from his jacket and touched the book. Nothing happened.

"It seems safe to take now. Let's go to the other exit. We still have intruders to deal with," said Marks.

"Sir, maybe we shouldn't take it out of here? I mean, it seems like a dangerous book. Is it possible you can just find the part you need and leave it here?" said Benson.

He has a point. An object this volatile is only inviting disaster.

"Take the book. I will need to read it thoroughly to find out how to protect the wards," said Marks.

Benson hesitated and then grabbed the book from the shelf. He paused a moment to see if anything would happen. When nothing occurred he breathed a sigh of relief. Benson tested the pages tentatively and opened the book.

"It seems safe now, sir. Do you want to take a look?" said Benson.

Unable to resist, Marks took the book. He thumbed through the first few pages until he saw a symbol he recognized. It was one of the major wards surrounding the park. He began to read a little more until he found the part about wards. The title was clear enough.

On the Protection or Destruction of Wardes.

Within the confines of the park I have commissioned to be constructed three stone towers (obelisks) which I have placed as amplifiers of the wardes surrounding the park grounds. Upon each sunrise the wardes are recharged and the energy is then distributed throughout the perimeter of the park. This maintains the integrity of the park containment.

Each tower is capable of maintaining the integrity on its own, thus a system of redundancy is created in the case of any breach, or the failing of the main wards. One tower must always remain standing.

These towers are crucial to the maintaining of the wardes, facilitating the continual use of solar energy into the wardes. If all three should fall the second failsafe must be instituted. On the matter of a breach, each of the towers must be recalibrated to the frequency of the perimeter. Failure to do so over a prolonged period of time will result in a catastrophic failure of the wardes guarding the park. Recalibration requires that the warde stones (as they have become known) be physically manipulated. This is a high risk proposition due to the denizens of the park. It is recommended that any such endeavor be undertaken in the light of the morning sun.-Calvert Vaux

"Benson, have you ever heard of anything called a ward stone?" said Marks. He began to wrap the book again as a tingling sensation crept through his hands. It seemed that the cloth only disabled the protective wards for a short period of time.

"No, sir, are they important?" said Benson.

"I would think so. Do we have a detailed map of the park?"

"Yes, sir, upstairs we have several maps of the park. Some of them are detailed," said Benson.

"Good. I need to see those maps and locate these stones --they are the key to keeping this city safe," said Marks. "Lead the way, Benson."

****

Gan found the panel he was looking for. He placed his hand on it and waited. The wards around the door disappeared and the door opened.

"How did you do that? I thought only an Overseer could drop those wards?" said Sepia.

"Or someone of an equal or higher clearance," said Gan.

"I thought you were retired, old man," said Cade.

"I am retired from active duty in the Order. I am still a ranking officer in the Grey. That gives me certain access," said Gan. "It also means that my presence here has been logged, which is never good for a Grey agent."

"I can see that being bad. Do you know where we are going?" said Sepia.

She checked her guns and holstered them. "This place sets my teeth on edge. Let's do this and get the hell out."

"We need to go to the Antiquities section if we need to find out about the wards. It should be over that way," said Gan.

Sepia and Cade looked around as they entered the Archives proper.

"I think I had that same look on my face when I first came down here," said Gan.

"How big is this place and how has it remained hidden?" said Sepia.

"It's huge. No one has given an accurate size of the place in the last ten years. It would probably take too long," said Gan.

Sepia and Cade stood transfixed.

"Okay, close your mouths and let's go. We need to get to the Antiquities section if we are going to learn about wards and how to keep them from failing," said Gan.

Gan led the way at a brisk walk. As they turned the corner leading to the Antiquities, they saw two figures.

"What the hell?" said Gan. He peered down the aisle and rocked back as the first shot caught him in the shoulder.

"Gun! Down, Cade!" exclaimed Sepia. The next few bullets missed Gan by inches.

"Pull him back, Blue. I have a bead on them," said Cade.

"Cade, shoot to wound--I need to know why they are down here," said Gan.

Cade stilled his breathing and looked at his targets.

"One is carrying a book. Hey, that looks like the guy that chased us in Queens," said Cade.

"Marks yes, that's him. It's the book we need, Cade. See if you can convince him to let it go," said Gan.

The words had barely left Gan's lips before Cade shot twice. One bullet grazed Marks in the hand, causing him to drop the book and run towards the exit Benson had shown him. The other shot caught Benson in the leg. Benson crashed to the ground grunting in pain.

Sepia ran over to where Benson lay and shoved him away from the book with her foot.

"Don't touch that book!" said Benson.

Sepia narrowed her eyes and pointed her sword at him.

"You or your boss just shot someone I care about a great deal. Give me a reason not to cause you a world of pain," she said.

"It wasn't me. It was Marks. I don't even carry-- you can check," said Benson.

Benson looked around nervously, making sure that Marks wasn't within earshot.

"Gan, is that you, sir?" he whispered.

Sepia turned to face Gan. "Do you know this guy?"

Gan nodded as he stood up. Cade dressed his wound and stopped the bleeding.

"Yes, I know him. Cade, take care of his leg," said Gan.

Cade hunched over Benson with his pack and placed some bandages on his leg. The bullet went right through the leg missing any major arteries.

"It's a good thing it was me who shot you -- someone else would have been sloppy and we would be trying to save your life now instead of dressing a wound."

Benson looked at Cade incredulously. "Is that encouragement?"

The leg dressed, Cade nodded, proud of his handiwork, and smiled. Then his face grew serious. He looked at Benson, his stare hard.

"I think you have some questions to answer," said Cade.

Sepia drew closer to the book that was now uncovered. She prodded it with her blade and managed to close it.

"What is this book and what were you doing with it?" said Sepia.

"That is a book on wards. It is one of many. That one is a journal and master text of ward creation and destruction," said Benson.

"And we just have this book lying around where anyone can access it?" said Sepia as she turned to Gan.

"It's not quite that simple. To get to this book requires Overseer clearance. Which means Marks is the new Overseer. Does he suspect you, Benson?" said Gan.

"I think he suspects everyone. If I hadn't told him about the cameras in the Archives I think he would have killed me down here," said Benson.

"What cameras? The Order never had cameras installed down here --too much interference to get a good video feed," said Gan.

"I know," said Benson

Gan smiled at him. "What is he planning? Do you know?"

"I know it has to do something to do with the wards. He kept saying they were the key to keeping the city safe. The last thing he asked about before you got here were something called the ward stones," said Benson.

"Ward stones? Does this book discuss those stones?" said Gan.

"Looks like it. First thing he asked about after he closed it –oh, that and detailed maps of the park," said Benson.

"How much time do we have?" said Sepia. She had wrapped the book with the cloth and now held it in her hands. "And we are taking this." She placed the book in her jacket pocket.

"I showed him where the auxiliary elevator is. He can get it running even with a breach in place. You have about an hour. When that elevator gets here it will be full of agents."

"This means we need to leave the way we came. Are you serious?" said Cade. "We are so fucked."

Gan turned to Benson.

"Against my better judgment, I'm going to leave you inserted. Do not underestimate him. He's intelligent and ruthless. He won't hesitate to end you if it serves his purpose," said Gan.

"I'll be careful, sir, and thank you sir," said Benson as he hobbled off, removing the bandages.

"What is he doing? I just stopped the bleeding," said Cade.

"It has to look real, Cade, or else his cover is blown," said Sepia.

Gan nodded. "I wonder how you made gunman sometimes, boy, seriously."

They headed out of the Archives at a run, conscious that time was against them.

"You think that behemoth is still out there waiting for us?" Cade said as they made their way down the tunnel.

"I hope so. If it's out there it means we will have less to deal with," she said.

"How bad is it when we are hoping for a behemoth to be outside waiting for us," said Cade.

"We need to get to Grey Command and that means going through the park at night without help. You need to focus, gunman," said Gan. His voice held a hard edge and Cade grew serious.

"Yes, sir. Let's make it happen," said Cade. They had reached the door at the end of the tunnel. On the other side, the park and the Unholy waited for them.

TWENTY-TWO

A CONTINGENT OF AGENTS poured out of the elevator once the doors opened. One of them opened a medical kit and treated Marks' hand. The others fanned out.

"They shot me and Benson. He's back there, if they left him alive," said Marks.

"Benson, sir?" asked one of the agents.

Marks waved the answer away.

"Go check the area near Antiquities --he should be around there somewhere."

Benson rounded the corner and hobbled over to where the agents stood. He counted close to fifteen agents. *The response team is impressive. Someone must be nervous,* thought Benson.

"I'm over here, sir. I couldn't stop them," said Benson.

"What was the reason for your presence down here, sir?" said the lead agent.

"The Overseer wished to become more familiar with the Archives in light of the heightened Nightmare activity in the city," said Benson.

The lead agent took down notes as Benson spoke.

"Why come down here to the Archives? I'm sure there are other ways to get information. The network, for instance, is a valuable resource," said the agent.

"The Overseer felt it has to do with the wards guarding the park." *In every lie let there be a grain of truth.* "So he thought this would be the best place to look for a solution," said Benson.

"Was anything removed from the Archives?" One of the agents asked. Marks looked at Benson, but his face betrayed no emotion.

"No, nothing was removed, we managed to surprise the intruders in the middle of whatever it was they were doing. I shot one and they returned fire, hitting us," said Marks.

The lead agent turned to face Benson. "Is that what happened?"

"Yes, that's what happened they came in through the old sewer line. They must have used some kind of explosive, considering the damage," said Benson.

"Why are you asking the same question again? The thieves are probably still in here. Go find them," said Marks.

"Yes, sir," said the lead agent. He didn't look convinced but followed the instructions given to him. The agents headed off in the direction of Antiquities leaving Marks and Benson alone with the medical personnel.

Marks didn't say anything and looked away from Benson. He appeared to be in deep thought as he made his way to the elevator.

"How is his wound?" said Marks to medic.

171

"He was lucky. An inch over to the left or right and he would have been done," said the medic.

"That was fortunate," said Marks.

The medic finished wrapping the wound in bandages then stood to make some notations in his tablet.

"Can you walk?" Marks said as he began to walk away.

Benson tested the leg and grimaced, more for effect than actual pain.

"I can manage. It's not too bad," he said.

"I don't think they will find anything, so let's head back up --we have things to plan," said Marks.

"Tell them I returned to my office. I expect a report of this activity on my desk within the hour," said Marks.

"Yes, sir," said the medic.

As the elevator doors closed Marks pressed his hand on the panel and the elevator began its ascent into the nexus of Home.

****

It was quiet in the tunnel. Gan started working on the locking mechanism. If something was waiting for them on the other side of the door he didn't want to attract its attention.

"How the hell are we going to get out of the park? Getting in is not a problem it's the getting out part that makes it fun," said Cade.

"Give me the book," said Gan. "You are going to have to push it tonight, Sepia. Once this door is open you draw your sword and you run as fast as you can for the edge of the park. We will go in the opposite direction."

172

"That's our plan? She's bait and we run in the other direction?" said Cade.

"Well, unless you want to be the bait? I don't think you will last out there long with the Unholy on your ass," said Gan.

"I don't like it, but we don't have a choice, do we?" said Cade. "Blue, you be careful, and don't stop for anything. Let me translate that for you. Haul ass until you are out of the park," said Cade.

Sepia handed the book to Gan, careful to keep it wrapped with the cloth.

"I'll go first and get their attention. Wait one minute and then you head east. I'm going to take them to the West side. Don't worry about finding me. I'll find you," she said.

She stepped out into the dark of the park. Tonight the hunter would be the hunted. She took a few steps and looked up into the night sky. The stars winked at her, oblivious to the danger she found herself in. For a moment she wished she could be up there, away from all of this. Then she heard the branches break. She drew her blade slowly and expanded her awareness.

"Let's go for a run," she said as she took off.

The first creatures she noticed were the wolves. They were on the fringe of her awareness closing fast behind her.

"I hate Dreadwolves," she said under her breath. The tattoos covering her body grew warm. In addition to protecting her from damage, they also gave her increased strength and stamina. This translated into her being able to push her body harder than a normal person. It also meant she could run fast --faster than a pack of Dreadwolves.

"She's got their attention. Let's hope she can keep it. Come on, boy, time to go," said Gan.

Gan and Cade left the tunnel and began running in the opposite direction from Sepia. In her awareness, she could sense them making their way across the park. She blocked that from her mind and focused on the task at hand. She needed to be more of a diversion. She started yelling and howling along with the wolves that chased her.

"That's bound to attract something," she said. She wasn't disappointed as the earth trembled slightly.

"Maybe it was too much of something," she muttered as she kept running.

It was the behemoth.

"What the hell was that, Gan?" said Cade.

"If I had to guess, I would say it was the behemoth that was waiting for us. Before you say it, we can't go back and we can't help her. She's a hunter, and a damned good one. She can handle this," said Gan as they made their way to the East side of the Park. *Be careful, blueberry.*

The behemoth was fast, faster than the wolves and it was getting closer. She ran faster than she thought possible. Her muscles were screaming at her and her ink flared keeping her warm and whole.

She soon realized out-running the behemoth wasn't going to be an option. She could hear Gan and Cade in her head telling her not to stop.

"No choice. I'm not going to run so I can die tired and exhausted," she muttered to herself as she slowed.

She stopped running and gathered herself. She didn't think she could match it in strength, but if it was chasing her sword, maybe she could fool it. She put the sword back in the scabbard and felt for the behemoth's location.

It slowed down and stopped and then started turning around in the opposite direction.

"Shit, the book! It probably does the same thing as my blade." She had no way of contacting them. Her coms were damaged after the fight with the siroc.

She drew her blade again and the behemoth turned toward her, giving chase again. It was close now. Close enough for her to hear its breathing.

"I can smell you, hunter," it said. "I can smell your fear. I will kill you slowly and then your friends after you."

Its voice cut through the night settling in the pit of her stomach. She felt fear, but it wasn't going to stop her. If she had to kill this creature to get out of the park alive, then she would kill it or die trying.

"Come get me, bitch." She held her sword before her and sensed its approach. *That can't be right. Why would it be up so high?* She rolled out of the way as it landed where she stood moments earlier, leaving an impact crater the size of a small van. Debris filled the air as the behemoth walked towards her.

"Hunter, you still don't understand? The time of humanity is coming to an end," said the behemoth. It picked up a boulder and hefted it in one hand.

"It's time to crush you like the insects you are. Tonight I'm going to start with you."

It threw the boulder with such velocity Sepia could only rely on reflex. She jumped to the side, avoiding the bulk of the large stone. The edge of the boulder clipped her in the shoulder and sent her spinning. Her ink flared and her arm hung lifeless. She stood up slowly, breathing hard.

"You think that hurt?" she said. "You must not have dealt with hunters. We don't quit, we don't lie down. We get shit done. Tonight, judging from your smell, you're the shit," said Sepia through clenched teeth. She was outclassed and she knew it, worse, the behemoth knew it and was toying with her.

The pain threatened to overwhelm her and the ground tilted for a second. Blood ran down her arm freely. The bones knitting themselves made her gasp in pain, catching her breath. She shifted forward and slashed at the behemoth. It stepped back, dodging the strike. Once out of range, she turned and ran. The behemoth began laughing behind her and started running. She pumped her legs as hard as she could. It felt like running in water--each step heavier than the last. Up ahead she saw the wall enclosing the park.

Her field of vision tunneled in and the edges grew dark. Her ink was coping with too much at once. The damage she was taking was overwhelming its ability to keep her functioning. In a few moments she would lose consciousness.

Wonder how many hunters died like that? Passing out in the middle of battle and getting finished. Seems like a flaw in the system, she thought as she ran. It was a skill that improved with time and experience. Over that time the ability to absorb greater damage increased. It also made the first few years of being a hunter the deadliest, for the hunter. *Just need to get to the wall.* Her vision was out of focus. She stumbled once and righted herself, moving faster. The behemoth landed in front of her blocking the wall.

"Where to now, little Hunter?" said the behemoth. Her shoulder was mobile now and she gripped her sword with both hands. The anger flared inside of her and her blade was covered with the black aura in the next second. It had never happened so fast, a part of her brain registered.

"You will get out of my way or die where you stand," she said.

Her voice had turned feral, and a guttural laughter escaped her lips. The behemoth cocked its head and looked uncertain. Her eye was glowing. She could see the light reflect off her blade, a dull green spilling into the night. It didn't matter. Nothing mattered as she charged the behemoth. She dove into its chest and buried her sword there with a double-handed thrust. The behemoth screamed in agony. She left the sword buried in the behemoth to the hilt as she back-flipped off it. The black aura remained on her hands as she advanced. The behemoth backed up, unsure what it was facing.

"I warned you," she said. She dashed in and pulled out the sword, and cut off one of its legs in the same stroke. The behemoth fell to the ground, groaning. Black liquid oozed from its chest and leg. It began laughing as it lay on the ground. Sepia stood over it, sword in hand.

"You are no hunter. You're one of us," it said as black liquid escaped its lips.

"I'm not one of you," Sepia whispered. "I'm worse."

Sepia brought the sword down and removed its head, kicking it away. The body slowly began to dissolve until nothing was left. She walked to the wall and slumped on the side. She grabbed the top and pulled herself over, falling to the ground on the other side.

"There she is. Was that a behemoth? I haven't seen one of those in years," said a voice.

The cool stone felt good against her face. She could see the first rays of dawn just peeking over the horizon. A shadow fell across her face and three figures surrounded her. They were all women, but not hunters.

"Sisters," Sepia managed before she passed out.

"She knows? Anna, how can she know?" said the sister who was crouched over Sepia's body. She was the smallest of the three.

"Asha, it doesn't matter what she knows," said Anna. Asha removed Sepia's guns and was about to remove the sword when Anna grabbed her hand.

"If you want to live to see the morning I suggest you leave that sword alone," said Anna.

Anna turned to the third sister who dwarfed them both.

"Pick her up, Alexa," said Anna. "Be careful not to touch the sword."

"Did she just face a behemoth alone?" said Asha.

"Yes, and no more talking. Our instructions are to bring her in," said Anna.

"How did she face it alone? Isn't she just a hunter?" said Asha.

"It would seem she is more than just a hunter," said Anna.

Alexa picked her up. They placed her in a waiting vehicle and drove off. Anna removed the scabbard and placed the sword in it, careful to avoid touching the blade.

****

Gan and Cade were outside of the park.

"Do you think she made it out okay?" said Cade.

"I'm sure she's fine. She knows most of the safe houses in the area. As soon as she can she will call. We need to get to Command and find out what we can do about the wards," said Gan.

Cade didn't answer but his gut told him something was wrong.

TWENTY-THREE

MARKS SAT AT THE HEAD OF the table in the conference room. On either side of him sat a total of fifteen men, motionless and quiet.

"Please send in Benson," said Marks into his intercom.

Benson walked in, his leg still stiff but no worse for wear.

"You wanted to see me, sir?" said Benson. He could see the maps on the table. Several areas were circled in red with notations next to them.

"Good morning, Benson. How's the leg?" said Marks.

"It's doing much better, sir. The medic gave me some painkillers and it's coming along," said Benson.

None of the men moved or acknowledged that Benson had entered the room. They may as well have been statues.

"I have a problem, Benson, that I would like your assistance with," said Marks.

"Anything, sir," said Benson. His gut told him this was a trap.

"Enthusiasm, I like that. Well, see, here is my problem. I don't trust you. Don't take it personally, I don't trust anyone except for these men. Do you see these men sitting here?" said Marks.

Benson looked around and knew the type: ex-military, skilled and highly trained. They offered blind loyalty with a generous dose of psychosis.

"Yes, sir, I see them," he said. He didn't like where the conversation was going.

"Any one of these men is willing to sacrifice their life for me. I trust them implicitly. You, however, I do not. Do you see my situation?" said Marks.

"No, sir, not really," said Benson.

"I can't have people close to me I can't trust. It complicates things," said Marks.

"Should I tender my resignation, sir?"

"That won't be necessary. I do have a solution however. One I think you will appreciate," said Marks.

"Yes, sir, anything I can do to help."

"These men will be going into the park to deal with the breach problem," said Marks.

"Have they located the stones?" asked Benson.

"They have pinpointed where the ward stones should be. After some aerial reconnaissance they will find the exact location of the stones and will try to repair them," said Marks.

"Aerial reconnaissance will be difficult, sir, given the nature of the park and the EMP field," said Benson.

"Didn't I tell you he would be useful?" Marks said looking at his men.

The men remained silent. "Yes, the field complicates matters so they will engage in limited runs. I'm told it should take a few days to find all of the stones. When that is done this insertion team will enter the park and fix the ward stones."

"I understand, sir. I don't see how I can help, sir. These men look trained for this kind of work," said Benson.

"Your help was instrumental in getting us to this point. I won't forget how you helped me in the Archives. You will be joining the team to make sure this mission goes off without a hitch," said Marks.

And to make sure I don't come back, thought Benson.

"Consider this a test of sorts, Benson. You pass this and I see good things in your future," said Marks.

"Yes, sir, I understand, sir." *My short future once we get inside the park. I have to get word to Gan somehow.*

"This man here is Roland Dietrich. He will be leading the team you are on. All your orders will be coming from him," said Mark.

Dietrich nodded to Benson. It was the only signal of acknowledgment he received.

"Please prepare your things. It looks like you will be entering the park in a few days. Should be plenty of time for your leg to heal," said Marks.

"Yes, sir, thank you for the opportunity to help in this matter," said Benson.

"No, Benson, thank you. By helping me you help the Order and the whole of this city," said Marks.

Benson left the conference room and headed to his office. He had planned for this contingency. Every Grey agent knew his life was on the line when taking an infiltration assignment. He would have to inform Gan of this mission before it was too late.

Once Benson left the conference room Marks stood and turned his back to the men sitting.

"Dietrich, I understand that this is a dangerous mission and that some of your men may not return from it. Make sure that Benson is one of those men. You're dismissed," said Marks.

The group of men stood and left the room without a sound.

This is shaping up to be a good week, thought Marks.

****

Gan and Cade were sitting across from Hep who was looking down at the book.

"This is some serious work. Way beyond me," said Hep.

"I'm not asking you to reproduce it, Hep, just figure out what we need to do with the wards. You have one hour," said Gan. He stood up and walked out of the armory.

"I've never seen him like that. I mean, sure he is always this side of high strung, but that's not like him. What's going on?" said Hep.

"It's Blue, she hasn't checked in and she isn't in any of the safe houses. He thinks it's the Sisters," said Cade.

Hep grew silent as he looked at the book before him.

"Also, the wards look like they will fail in about a year, which means the Unholy will be on the streets of the city. Basically the end of life as we know it," said Cade.

"If the Sisters have her, I'm not going to lie to you, it's not good. They are the best at what they do. They fulfill contracts and kill," said Hep. "I can't help you with that. With this, I can help," he said as he pointed down at the book.

"You know what those designs mean?" said Cade.

"They are a variation of the wards that contain the park. These are a bit nastier, though, which means that whoever placed them didn't want the wrong people reading this book," said Hep.

"How are they different? They look like the same designs over and over," said Cade.

182

"You see this design here--the one that looks like a figure eight? See how it's repeated in several locations?" said Hep.

Cade nodded. He had noticed the same design on the walls of the park. "Yeah, those symbols are all over the park walls. What are they?"

"They maintain the integrity of the ward. Usually it's for a fixed period of time. Wards degrade over time, but not these. These can go on indefinitely. This work is incredible," said Hep.

"So is this book dangerous?" said Cade. He wondered if it was worth the price of leaving his hunter out there.

"It's dangerous and valuable. I really need to get to it," said Hep.

"I understand. Hope you can find anything that will help us in there."

Cade left the armory and headed for the main floor. It was bustling with activity and he could see Gan surrounded by several agents. Gan motioned him over.

"The Sisters have her. We were able to pick it up on some of the cams we have stationed across from the park," said Gan.

"Those things work that close to the park?" said Cade.

"They have shielding and the wards actually help believe it or not," said Gan.

"Where is she? Where did they take her?" said Cade.

"I have people working on that and as soon as I know, you will. I promise. Why don't you try and get some rest. We can't do anything else until we know more," said Gan. He placed a hand on Cade's shoulder and ushered him out of the nexus. An agent waited to take him to sleeping quarters.

"We'll find her. Go get some shuteye. You're no use to anyone exhausted," said Gan.

"Okay, old man. As soon as you know anything you get me," said Cade.

"You have my word. Don't worry, Sepia is trained and she is a hunter. The Sisters have their hands full," said Gan.

****

Sepia opened her eyes and found herself bound to the bed she was on. The room was sparsely furnished but well maintained. She pulled against the bonds and found them secure enough to hold her.

"Don't bother. Those bonds will hold you until I say otherwise," said a female voice. She had a slight accent Sepia couldn't place.

Sepia looked around for the speaker and found her seated across from the foot of the bed. Sepia moved into a seated position and faced the woman. She was older than Sepia, her short hair peppered with gray and revealed a strong jaw line. Sepia could tell she trained regularly. Her body-- while thin--was defined. She was looking at the body of a warrior.

"My name is Anna. I am the current head of a group you may know as the Sisters. You have me in quite the position," said Anna.

"Where are my weapons?" Sepia rasped. Her throat felt sore and her body felt bruised.

"There's some water on the table beside you," said Anna. "As for your weapons, they are safe."

"My blade, don't let anyone draw it," said Sepia.

"I am well aware of the properties of a named blade, hunter. No one has or will attempt to use your blade. Please drink some water," said Anna.

Sepia reached for the cup and found she could reach it. She drank the cool water in small sips.

"If you are feeling pain, I apologize. The bonds around your wrists negate the properties of your ink," said Anna. "It was a precaution I'm sure you can understand, considering your abilities."

"That would explain the feeling of swallowing glass," said Sepia.

"On that subject, which artist worked on you? I rarely see a hunter done so extensively and with such a level of skill. It is the work of an ink master," said Anna with admiration.

"I honestly don't remember. It was someone my mother knew and it was done when I was still young," said Sepia as she looked at her arms. She saw no reason to lie to this woman, considering her position.

"May I ask your mother's name?"

"My mother's name was Emiko. Emiko Tanaka," said Sepia. "Did you know her?"

"I knew of her. Your mother, was one of the first female hunters. They were known as the terrible twenty. Your mother was called the Jade Demon. She had a fearsome reputation and was expected to die in the field on her first day. She gave them quite a surprise," said Anna with a smile.

"I think I got some of that from her."

"Indeed. Well that would explain the level of artistry in your ink. She would only let one person work on her daughter, I'm sure. Which means your work is the product of the famed ink master, Zanshin," said Anna.

"Doesn't sound familiar," said Sepia.

"That wasn't his real name of course, but it was the only name he went by. He's been dead now for over twelve years. This makes you mid-thirties?" said Anna.

"Thirty- three, actually, and this is relevant because?" said Sepia.

"Because of the position I am in, hunter. The Sisters never renege on a contract, ever," said Anna. Her voice was steel, cutting every syllable.

"Who put the contract on me?" said Sepia.

"Does it matter? It came through the proper channels," said Anna.

"It matters because in less than a year the wards will fail completely. If that happens there won't be a group of Sisters to worry about. All the Unholy will be released. A rogue hunter will be the least of your problems," said Sepia. She was taking a chance that Anna cared more for her Sisters than the fulfillment of a contract.

"That would explain the presence of the behemoth certainly, but it is not enough. Proof, get me proof of this and perhaps we can make an exemption. Otherwise, these are just words," said Anna.

"Do you have a secure line I can call from?" said Sepia.

Anna's eyes narrowed as she tossed a phone on the bed next to Sepia. *Stupid question. These are world class assassins, of course they have a secure line,* thought Sepia.

Sepia used one hand to dial Gan. It rang once and he picked up.

"Where are you? Where are you calling from?" said Gan. Anna took the phone from Sepia.

"Hello, Ganriel, it has been a long time since we have spoken," said Anna.

"No one calls me that anymore, Anna. Where do you have Sepia?" said Gan.

"A contract was placed with us for her. The terms were dead or alive, although the client didn't mind having her dead. Why is that, Ganriel? Why is this hunter so dangerous? I have seen many who have greater skill than this one," said Anna turning to face Sepia as she spoke.

"It would seem she has powerful enemies. Not many have the ability to issue you a contract," said Gan. "Can I use my right of dispensation?"

"Do you know the cost? This is not a matter to be taken lightly," said Anna.

"Don't do it, Gan. Whatever it is I'll figure a way out!" exclaimed Sepia.

"Silence, hunter, your life is hanging in the balance and he bargains with his own," said Anna.

Sepia glared at Anna but kept silent.

"Very well, Ganriel, but before we discuss the terms tell me about the wards," said Anna.

Gan told her about the imminent failing of the wards and what that would mean for the city and the world if they did.

"The hunter told me as much, but I require proof that what you say is true. Do you have any?" said Anna.

"Grant me the dispensation on her contract and I will give you the proof," said Gan.

"Very well, I will grant dispensation for Sepia Blue, daughter of Emiko Tanaka. Her contract is to be undertaken by you, Ganriel. You have a month," said Anna. "Upon my word as bond."

"One more thing, Anna," said Gan.

"You are placing conditions on a dispensation with me? You have not changed one bit, Ganriel," said Anna, furious.

"Yes I am, because of our past and our history and for the number of times I saved your life," said Gan.

Anna's faced softened. "You know I cannot change the time allotted, that is beyond me. The contract must be fulfilled. It is our way," said Anna.

"I am asking for neither. I request that she be accepted into the Sisters with my vote of confidence. She is blacklisted with the hunters and cannot return, even if I clear her name. The suspicions will linger. As a Sister she will at least have a home after I am gone," said Gan.

"She is not trained in our ways, Ganriel. She is barely an adequate hunter, although I do see some promise. The training will kill her," said Anna.

"I only ask you give her the chance. The rest is up to her," said Gan.

"On your vote I will allow her to enter the training. If she passes she will be one of us. Upon my word as bond," said Anna.

"I accept your word as bond. Thank you, Anna. This means everything to me," said Gan. "I will have one of my men pick Sepia up. Please send me the location. Once Hep is done I will send you our proof. It is a warded book, along with documentation regarding the breaches. Do you remember the handling of those?" said Gan.

"As long as it has its protective covering, yes I know how to handle it," said Anna.

"Until I see you again, or you see me," said Gan. He hung up the phone. It was an old expression among assassins. The next time they met, one would die.

"What did he do? What is a dispensation?" Sepia said from the bed. She didn't like the sound of it.

Anna didn't answer right away. She sat on the bed with her back to Sepia.

"Ganriel was a good friend once, long ago. We fought alongside each other many times," said Anna.

"What do you mean was? What did he do?"

She struggled against the restraints, but it was pointless.

"A dispensation is a special clause in the Sisters contract. If the person has the authority in the Order they can call for a dispensation. They take on the contract as if they are the target, freeing the intended target."

"No, he didn't. Tell me he didn't do that," said Sepia in a whisper.

"He did. You must be very special to him. A dispensation gives the new target a month to get their affairs in order and then the contract is fulfilled," said Anna. "A dispensation can only occur once in a contract and is irreversible. Once the word of a Sister is given, it is law."

"What about the rest, the part about the training killing me? What was his condition?" said Sepia.

"He requested you be allowed to join the Sisters, since you are no longer welcome among the hunters."

"I can't believe he did this. Why did he do this?"

"You can ask him yourself when you see him. He is sending a car over to get you," said Anna.

"Has anyone ever escaped one of the Sisters contracts?" said Sepia.

189

"No one in the recorded history of the Sisters has ever escaped a contract that was issued against them. However, if there is one man who can do it, Ganriel is that man. I wish him luck," said Anna. "If you will excuse me, I have to inform our client that the contract will be delayed by a month."

Anna stood and headed for the door.

"Can you tell me who the client is? Do you still fulfill the contract if there is no client?" said Sepia.

Anna turned, a wry smile on her face.

"I can see some of what he sees in you. Of course I cannot share that information with a hunter. It would violate one of our oldest precepts," said Anna.

Sepia sighed, frustrated. She pleaded with her eyes.

"However, since you are to undergo our training that would make you a Sister novitiate. I can share that information with a Sister," said Anna. She held the back of the chair and leaned forward as she spoke.

"If I were to guess, I would look at those who had the Authority to contract us. It requires Overseer clearance and above. Have you made enemies of any Overseers recently?"

Anna walked out of the room and left Sepia with her thoughts.

TWENTY-FOUR

A FEW MOMENTS LATER TWO women entered the room. Sepia recognized them as two of the women she saw at the park. The smaller of the two carried all her weapons. Once her restraints were removed, her ink restored her body and she felt fully recovered.

"Hello, my name is Asha. These are yours."

It was looking at two extremes. Where Asha was small and waif-like, Alexa was large and muscular.

Asha gently placed the weapons on the bed. Sepia checked her guns and saw they were loaded. *I guess shooting them would be in bad form.* She holstered her guns and slung her blade over her shoulder and back.

"Thank you. Did anyone try to, you know, touch my blade?" said Sepia as she strapped the leather ties to her body.

"I was tempted, back at the park. Anna said it was a bad idea," said Asha.

"Do you always do what Anna says?" said Sepia.

Asha cocked her head to one side and Alexa laughed quietly behind her.

"Have you met Anna? She is the leader of the Sisters. That's not an honorary title. She had to fight to get that position. Yes, I do everything Anna says," said Asha.

"So it's out of fear, then?" said Sepia. She was beginning to dislike this group more and more by the second. *What the hell did you get me into, Gan?*

"No, not fear, respect. We all respect her because she looks out for us. She cares for us and makes sure we are ready. She's hard but fair. You really can't ask for more than that in this life," said Asha.

Alexa nodded as she pulled out a blindfold and held it in both hands.

Sepia understood that feeling more than most and looked at the two women with begrudging respect. "I'm ready to go," said Sepia. Alexa stepped over and placed the blindfold over her eyes.

Asha grabbed Sepia's hand and led her to the underground garage.

"Soon you won't need the blindfold, you'll be one of us," said Asha as she closed the vehicle door and they pulled off.

They were outside. Sepia could feel the cool breeze as she stepped out of the vehicle. It was morning. The heat of the sun warmed her face. The blindfold was removed and she stood on the corner of street facing Columbus Circle as a black SUV pulled up. Cade was at the wheel. Several Grey agents rode in the SUV. They all had weapons drawn and looked ready to go at a moment's notice. Sepia got in the passenger side and looked behind her. The agents looked tense.

"What gives?" said Sepia.

Cade looked her over and smiled as he brushed his hair with his hand.

"How was your vacation with the Sisters?" said Cade.

"Restful. Want to tell me why they all look like a Nightmare is about to pounce on them?" said Sepia. Cade flipped down the visor on the passenger side and Sepia saw her reflection in the mirror. Her left eye gave off a green glow.

"Shit, I don't have my glasses," said Sepia as she checked her jacket pockets.

Cade handed her a pair of her wraparounds, which she put on.

"You could have said something you know," said Sepia.

Cade was adjusting the rearview mirror and laughing. "And miss the expression on these guys? Oh, hell no. This is priceless," said Cade.

"I've had a rough night, can we get back to Gan? I need to speak to him now," said Sepia.

"Rough night? You were MIA for three days, Sepia. Gan was about to rip the city in half when he got your call," said Cade.

"Three days?" said Sepia. *How can I have been out for three days?*

"You don't remember? You were fighting a big ugly thing, the behemoth?" said Cade. He gave her sidelong glances as he drove down Broadway.

"I remember the Behemoth --no way I can forget that thing," said Sepia. She also remembered its last words. *You're one of us,* it taunted her. *I have never blacked out for that long. It is getting worse.*

"And stop looking at me like that, I'm fine. I just didn't think it was that long," said Sepia.

"Well, while you were on vacation, it has been getting dicey out here. Another Behemoth was seen two nights ago at the edge of the park. Last night one was sighted just outside," said Cade.

"It's like they're testing the strength of the wards," said Sepia.

"Gan was thinking the same thing. We have a team going into the park today to see if we can find something called ward stones. These stones are supposed to make sure the wards don't fail. At least that's what Hep says," said Cade.

"How many on this team?" she said.

" 'Teams.' We are one of three. Each team has a hunter pair in it. We get the lowest stone, around Seventieth Street. The other two are midway in the park and at the top. It's one team for each stone," said Cade.

"Why now? I thought we had close to a year?" said Sepia.

"Gan's man on the inside says Marks is planning something with the ward stones. For some reason Gan doesn't trust Overseer Marks. I am inclined to agree with him," said Cade.

"We aren't going to see Gan, are we?" said Sepia.

Cade didn't answer her.

"What did he tell you? He told you not to take me to command." She was getting angry now.

"He said it made no point discussing what was done. We need you here. You're one of the best hunters out here."

"That stubborn old man. You don't know what he did," she said.

"You know you can't change his mind anyway. Stubborn doesn't even begin to define him," said Cade.

"You and I are going to have some words when we get back," said Sepia.

"If we get back," said Cade with a smile.

"Aren't you the fucking optimist," said Sepia.

Cade laughed as Sepia looked out the passenger side window. A small smile crept across her face.

They drove in silence until Cade pulled up to the 68th Street entrance.

"This is us. Let me contact the other teams," said Cade. He input some commands on the dashboard computer and all of the teams were connected via their coms.

"I didn't know we could do that. That would make patrolling much easier," said Sepia.

"We can do this only because we are so close. Once we enter the park we will lose the other teams. Each one is on its own," said Cade.

"This is Alpha. We are in position," said Cade.

"This is Beta. Roger that, we are in position," said a female.

"This is Omega. We are in position and ready to go," said a female. Sepia recognized that voice: Red Jen.

"Red Jen? She hates my guts," whispered Sepia.

"She's good and she is about fifty blocks away. It's a non-issue. Let's focus, Blue," said Cade.

"You're right." She nodded apologetically. "What's the plan?" said Sepia.

"According to Hep, we get to the ward stone and each hunter realigns the stone then we get the hell out. Sounds like a walk in the park," said Cade.

"How am I supposed to align the ward stone? Did Hep go into that?" said Sepia.

"I was getting to that. You weren't at the briefing or you would know this already. You need to insert your sword into a placeholder in the ward stone, and align through the stone. That's supposed to do it," said Cade.

"How long is that supposed to take, Cade? It's not like we have all day here. This is the park remember? Full of the Unholy who want us dead?" said Sepia.

"I don't know how long it takes, that's why I'm coming with. Hep couldn't get that info from the book. Bottom-line is we do this, the wards don't fail and we get to have a nice city with the Unholy contained. We fail, it's game over," said Cade.

"Then let's make sure we don't fail," said Sepia.

"Okay, Hep tells me these coms will work in the park on burst transmissions only. That means lag time between your transmission and any response," said Cade.

"So basically we're on our own," said Red Jen.

"Pretty much, yeah," said Cade.

"That just the way I like it. Try not to fuck this up Sepia," said Red Jen.

"Beta is going in. We'll see you on the other side" said the female.

"Who's on Beta? She sounds familiar," said Sepia.

"That's Lisa and Xavier. Gan called them in," said Cade. "Jen got some new guy, since she lost her gunman recently. His name is Charles--goes by Chuck," said Cade.

"This is Omega. We're going in," said Red Jen.

That must mean that Gan called in three named blades for this op, thought Sepia.

"This is Alpha. We're going in," said Cade "Good luck, people. Remember, no cavalry is coming to save our asses," said Cade.

"No one would want to save your ass anyway, it's too ugly," said Xavier.

"Yours isn't much better X," said Lisa. Laughter erupted on the coms.

"What was that about the doctors slapping your face when you were born? Some kind of confusion there, X?" Cade said as they exited the truck. Sepia and Cade walked into the park. Sepia felt the crossing of the wards like an electrified field.

"Gan's not pulling any punches," said Sepia as they walked in.

"This is it, Blue. If we blow this, poof there goes New York, there goes the U.S. and it's only a matter of time before it's another Unholy war everywhere," said Cade. All mirth was gone from his voice now. His only focus was the mission and its completion.

"What's the worst case scenario?" she said.

"You mean besides the one I just described where we all die and the world is overrun by the Unholy?" said Cade.

"Yes, besides that one. I'm talking about the aligning of the ward stones. What happens if we can't align them?"

"Hep says a secondary failsafe kicks in, but he didn't find out what it was. When I left him he was still in that book," said Cade.

"This is the best shot we have. We have to take it. I for one do not want to see another Unholy War start because we fucked up," said Cade.

"Neither do I. I'm just concerned about the alignment part. This thing with the blade has been getting dicey," she said.

The park looked idyllic. The sun streamed through the leaves and Sepia could envision a past when people walked on the paths to enjoy their days. It was sad that such a beautiful place was home to such ugliness. *We did that. We caged them in here. If I was a Nightmare I would be pissed too. A jail is still a jail even if it's beautiful.* She shook her head clear of the thought.

"You okay? According to the map, says we have under a click to go, that way," said Cade as he pointed northeast."

The silence of the park fell on them like a warm blanket.

"Something's off, Cade. The park is never this quiet," said Sepia.

"This is Omega! We have company. These guys look like Order mercs." It was Red Jen.

"This is a fucking ambush! My gunman is down, repeat, Charles is down. Shit," said Jen. "These guys are doing something to the ward stone. Applying some kind of paste to it," said Jen.

197

Gunfire erupted in the background and then the com went silent.

"This is Beta. I've got eyes on five on the ground around the stone. I don't know how they got here before us," said Xavier. Silenced gunfire followed and Xavier came through the com again.

"These guys are trained. I only managed to drop two before they took cover. They were doing the same thing, some kind of paste on the stone," said Xavier over the sound of rifle fire.

"It's Marks, he sent those guys in. He doesn't want to fix the wards he wants to destroy them!" exclaimed Sepia, running toward the last ward stone.

"Sepia, wait, don't rush in!" said Cade as he ran after her. They found the obelisk standing alone.

"This is Alpha. Our stone is clear. Examining the stone now," said Cade.

Sepia walked around the ward stone. It stood close to seven feet tall and was covered in symbols. On one side of the obelisk, the symbols surrounded the shape of a sword.

"These symbols, Cade, I can read them," said Sepia.

"What does it say?"

She pointed to one symbol and then another.

"This one here means 'blade'. This one means 'protector'. That other one means 'joined'," said Sepia. "I think it's referring to the aligning of the stone."

She drew her blade and the obelisk began to hum.

"Let's go, no reason to think they won't be coming for this one too. Do what we came to do," said Cade.

Another burst in on the com. "This is Omega. The paste is some kind of acid –it's dissolving the stone. I repeat, acid on the stone," said Jen. "I'm heading out. I have four on me. I'm going to ground and taking them out. Get it done, rookie." More gunfire erupted in the background and then silence.

Sepia stood in front of the stone and was about to place her sword in the shape on the obelisk when Cade pulled her down to the ground forcing the air out of her lungs.

"Can't let you do that, little lady," said Dietrich.

Sepia looked up to see the bullet hole in the obelisk where her head was seconds earlier.

"Thanks," she whispered.

"Don't thank me yet, these guys look like they're serious," said Cade.

Cade rolled over to the side to get to a flanking position. "I'm going to get their attention; you do what you need to do."

Cade began firing as Sepia stood and placed the sword in the obelisk. The sword remained fixed in the obelisk as if magnetized. She waited a moment.

Nothing happened. Sepia looked at Cade who stared at her in disbelief. They both looked at the obelisk.

"You failed, hunter. Drop your weapons, gunman, before I tell my men to kill you where you stand," said Dietrich. The men began to walk closer to them. Cade dropped his guns.

"Sepia, now would be a good time to, you know, align?" said Cade out of the corner of his mouth.

Sepia calmed her breath and reached out to her sword. Power flooded her body. Her awareness expanded until she could sense the entire park, every tree, every blade of grass, every stone and pebble. She was rapidly going into sensory overload. It was too much for her brain to process. The ground began to tremble and the obelisk began to sink into the ground. The sword hovered in the air before her as she stood at the epicenter of a shockwave that rocked the area around her. Cade managed to pick up his guns as he, Dietrich and his men were flung to the side.

Her awareness snapped back to her body and she focused on her blade. She placed a hand on her blade and it liquefied, pouring into her hand, disappearing. Then the wards dropped.

****

"Do you feel that, witch? The wards guarding this pen have fallen," said Chimera. "It's only a matter of time now before I am rid of you."

Calisto could feel the wards around the keep weakening.

"This can't be. How could they fail?" said Calisto.

"Because they are human, and like all humans they function best when told what to do. What more do you expect from cattle?" said Chimera.

"They cannot fail," Calisto whispered. Despair crept into her voice as she thought the unimaginable. The world would fall to the Unholy. Humanity would be slaughtered for sport. It was the end of everything.

Chimera stepped close to her side and spoke into her ear.

"They can and they have. I feel stronger with every passing second," said Chimera. "In fact, I think I'm going to go for a stroll." Chimera opened the door to the keep and stepped outside. The wards surrounding the Keep flickered and flared. Chimera looked down and saw them slowly fade away. He took a step over the threshold and stood past the area where the wards had been.

"This is our time now. Humans just became an endangered species. They just don't know it yet," said Chimera.

Calisto could only look on from inside the keep. Even now she felt her power fading away. If she dared to go outside she would be gone. *Even in this form I cling to life. I must warn the others.* She walked outside, growing weaker with each step. She stopped at the threshold that no longer contained wards. Chimera now several feet away turned back and smiled at her, his eyes shifting hue.

"Do you feel it, witch? Power, raw power. The ward stones have been destroyed and now that power is mine."

Calisto felt the power and underneath it a current of something else. The wards began to glow beneath her feet and she smiled. Her power returned.

"You were a bit premature, Chimera. You may have escaped this keep but you have not left the park yet," said Calisto. The wards continued to increase in intensity until they were bright amber, burning into the ground and solidifying.

"No, no! We are so close! I will not be defeated, not now," said Chimera. He turned and focused on the source of the power. He closed his eyes and Calisto could see the energy coalesce around his body.

"What are you doing?" said Calisto, alarmed. The energy was so great she could feel its presence move her back.

"Ahh, there she is, and she has aligned the stone and her sword. This is my moment to strike. Good bye, witch, in time I will return to erase you and this wretched keep from my grounds. Right now I have a hunter to kill."

His eyes were twin orbs of green fire as he looked at her and laughed. She took several steps back unsure if the wards surrounding the keep could stop him.

"My brethren and I will be free today, witch," he said as he ran towards Sepia's location.

Calisto could feel the wards of the Park begin to reassert their presence. It was the slow buildup of a wave gaining force and momentum. If he struck before they were fully reformed they were all doomed.

****

Sepia felt the power coursing through her. Her blade was in her, part of her now. The ward stone was channeling energy through her sword, through her. She placed her hands on the floor and the obelisk began to rise again. Higher and higher it went until it stopped at fifty feet.

"Sepia, I don't think this is a good place to be right now. Maybe we should back up," said Cade. Dietrich and his men had retreated away from the obelisk that now towered over them.

Sepia ignored Cade and drew closer to the ward stone. It was a magnetic attraction. The power called to her. Her left eye flared a green flame as she took each step.

"It's the power. It calls to you. Embrace it, accept it. This is who you are, what you are. You are one of us," said Chimera.

"Weapons free, men!" shouted Dietrich. "Cut them down!"

"Excuse me a moment," said Chimera. The bullets had no effect on him. Cade noticed that they were being stopped before they reached the Nightmare Lord. As Chimera turned to face the shooters he swept his arms with the fingers extended. It was a casual gesture. A green wave shot across the ground rushing toward Dietrich and his men. Cade sprinted away and dove behind some trees, barely escaping it. Dietrich and his men were enveloped in green energy, which slowly broke their bones as it crept up their bodies. Their screams echoed through the park.

"Now, where was I?" said Chimera as he turned back to Sepia. She was transfixed before the ward stone, the power a palpable force enveloping her.

Cade had evaded the wave of destruction. He could see Dietrich and his men spasm as their bodies contorted, suspended a foot above the ground, bones breaking.

"Shit. That's inhuman." He shot Dietrich's men in the forehead before they went through more agony. He left Dietrich for last. Dietrich didn't cry out, even though the pain must have been unbearable.

"Thank you," said Dietrich a moment before Cade put a bullet between his eyes.

If Chimera realized what happened he gave no indication. He was focused on Sepia.

"C'mon, Sepia, snap out of it. Don't let him win," said Cade to himself.

"It's wondrous. With this power no one could stand before you. You could rule. Take it, it is your birthright," said Chimera.

He's right-- with this power no one could touch me. I would be invincible. I wouldn't need the Order or the Sisters or anyone.

Sepia, her hands on the stone began siphoning more power into her body. Blood flowed from her ears and nose. Her ink flared but she kept drawing more. The power was too much for her body to contain and still she drew more. She couldn't stop.

"Yes, you see it now, don't you? This power is yours. It belongs to you. Take it all. Surrender to it, let it enter you completely," said Chimera.

"I hope she forgives me for this," said Cade. He took aim with his rifle and put Sepia in his sights. Taking a deep breath, he squeezed the trigger. The bullet dug a groove in her cheek as it continued on its trajectory past her. She placed a hand on her face, breaking the connection to the ward stone. Chimera took a step back and looked in Cade's direction.

"No more interference from you," said Chimera. He extended his hand and the air around Cade began to solidify, crushing him. Sepia was still dazed and shook her head.

"Blue, wake up!" said Cade. It was his last breath. He fell to the ground, clutching at his neck, unable to breathe.

"Leave him alone," said Sepia, still uncertain.

"He is nothing --a speck of insignificant dust," said Chimera.

"Leave him alone," said Sepia.

"Do you see how he squirms? He is not worthy of breathing the same air as you. I am actually doing him a favor, ending his pitiful existence," said Chimera.

Cade's face was mottled as he thrashed on the ground trying to breathe. Sepia slammed her fist into the side of Chimera's head, sending him back several feet. Cade lay motionless, but breathing.

"I said, leave him alone," said Sepia.

Chimera rubbed his jaw as he faced Sepia.

"What? Do you care for that? He is dirt, less than dirt!"

"He is my friend, my family. You don't fuck with my family," said Sepia. She clenched her hands into fists.

Chimera rubbed the side of his head and smiled.

"You should have never taken your hand off the ward stone. Your end would have come and you would have died basking in power as your body melted away. Not a bad way to go, all things considered. Now I have to kill you. That will involve large amounts of pain, for you," said Chimera.

The ward stone began to vibrate as the energy build up increased. Blue-white energy raced up the top of the stone until it formed a large sphere at the apex. The sphere grew to four feet in diameter and exploded, sending several shards of energy in every direction. Sepia looked up and saw two shards head into the park. As she was watching the trajectory of the shards she didn't notice the shard that was headed for her. It entered her body and suffused it with light. The awareness of the park returned but it was subdued. It didn't overwhelm her senses. Behind her, the ward stone cracked and crumbled and fell to the earth as it reverted to dust.

"I see. The secondary protocol has been initiated. You hunters are now the keepers of the wards, through your blades. This just makes it easier. I only have to kill hunters and we will be free. I am going to enjoy this," said Chimera.

TWENTY-FIVE

SEPIA'S BODY CRACKLED WITH ENERGY as she absorbed the shard. The light from her left eye flared in the night, bathing the ground in green light.

"Do you need more proof that you are closer to my kind than theirs? Have you seen yourself? You look absolutely nightmarish," said Chimera.

The increased power threatened to undo Sepia. Chimera laughed at her struggle for control.

"You don't control this kind of power, child. You let it have free reign. You give it access to all of you," he whispered.

"I am going to end you," said Sepia.

"You can most certainly try," said Chimera as he opened his arms wide.

Sepia extended her arm and her sword slowly coalesced in her hand. Its blade had tinges of green now that shifted and moved.

"Another Jade Demon? I remember watching the first one die. Killing you will be just as pleasurable," said Chimera.

Sepia was rocked to her core. This creature was responsible for her mother's death.

"You killed her? But you aren't a T8," said Sepia.

Chimera looked at her and laughed. It was an evil and cruel sound, full of hatred.

"You are a stupid child. I was never a T anything! You have not seen power of this magnitude. It was the same mistake she made, believing the assessment of her gunman and trusting others. That misplaced trust is what killed her," said Chimera.

"I am not your child," she said.

Sepia was full of rage. She ran toward Chimera holding her sword to her side. At the last second she swung her blade up into Chimera. She met his sword instead.

The sound echoed through the trees. He shoved her attack to the side and lunged. She managed to evade his attack with a counter and a shift of her body. His sword looked rapier-thin, but she could see the edges were sharp. The entire blade was covered in a dark aura that came off the sword in waves and dissipated into the air.

Their swords locked, he drew close and whispered, "All that power could have been yours alone. It's still not too late."

"It also would have killed me," she grunted with the effort. He was so strong.

"Nothing of value comes without a cost," he said. He kicked her in the midsection and sent her flying back. She landed on her back and quickly recovered, springing to her feet. He closed the distance with a flurry of attacks. Her defense was failing. She rolled back to get some breathing room but he pressed his attack. As he lunged, she miscalculated the distance and turned too late. His thrust sliced her midsection and she began to bleed. Her ink didn't flare to protect her and fear filled her eyes. She clutched her wound, blood filling her hand.

"Now you are beginning to understand, hunter. Your ink will not protect you in here with me and this," he said as he raised his sword at her. She could feel her ink working, just slowly. *The energy from his sword must be suppressing my ink,* she thought.

"Just accept it, hunter. As deaths go, you could do worse," said Chimera.

"I may die today, but not before you," she said.

She attacked with a feint to his right and struck left. He saw through the feint and was waiting for her on the right with a fist to her jaw. She fell back, dazed.

"Pathetic. It is clear you were trained by an amateur," said Chimera. Her awareness registered another person close to them. It wasn't Cade.

"I see I don't have your full attention," said Chimera as his hand began to glow. "Let me rid you of all distractions so you can focus on your imminent death."

He sent a blast of energy toward the prone body of Cade. A figure jumped in front of the blast and was sent flying back. It was Benson.

Chimera laughed as Benson lay dying. A large wound soaked his chest in blood.

"How noble and how pointless. You make my task that much easier by throwing your lives away for each other," said Chimera.

"No more," whispered Sepia.

Sepia clenched her fists and her sword receded back into her body.

"It is time to accept the inevitability of your position. This is a wise choice, hunter," said Chimera.

He lunged, a killing blow. She reached out and grabbed his sword, stopping it mid-thrust. The blade dug into her hand, cutting her, and still she held on. The dark energy surrounding his blade crept up her arms and she laughed. Her eye flared bright green as she extended one arm. Pulling on his sword she jerked him forward toward her. Instantly her sword appeared in her other hand. She sliced horizontally across his neck.

"That's not possible. How could you withstand my blade?"

"No more killing," said Sepia.

His sword fell to the ground as he took several steps back. His head fell to the side with a look of surprise on his face. She kicked the head away from the body and ran toward Benson and Cade. Chimera's body did not dissolve.

"Benson, don't move. You're going to be okay," she knew it was a lie the moment she saw his wound. He saw the expression on her face.

"It's okay. Occupational hazard," he tried to laugh but it came out as a rough cough instead.

"Don't you die on me, I'll get help." She moved to stand and he grabbed her hand, stopping her.

"It's too late. I had a good run. Tell Gan it was an honor. I sent him all the information I could gather."

"Benson. She knew there was nothing she could do. "Thank you, thank you for saving Cade."

"It was the least I could do," he said and then died.

Tears ran down her face as the anger filled her and she fell to her knees. She raged against the senseless deaths, the loss of her friends, her family. She didn't notice when the scream began but it became the only thing, the center of her world. Nothing else mattered anymore. Her entire being was in that scream. It was release, it was rage, and it was surrender. The ground around her began to liquefy as she was engulfed in green fire.

"Sepia! Sepia, come back!" It was a distant voice on the edge of her consciousness. She turned and looked around and saw the figure standing there. She knew this man.

"It's me, Blue, just come on back. You can do it," said Cade in a measured tone.

Gradually the flames receded and went out. Sepia stood in the middle of a charred circle of earth.

"What the hell happened?" said Sepia.

She was disoriented and fell to the ground, exhausted. Cade came over slowly and lifted her to her feet.

"Everything hurts," she said.

"For a moment there I thought I'd lost you. You had a meltdown, in the worst sense," said Cade.

Cade looked around and saw the body of Benson. He looked questioningly at Sepia.

"He died saving you," she said.

Cade nodded his understanding and picked up the body, moving it away from the charred circle.

"Now what?" she said.

"The wards are back in place, you took care of their boss. I would say this was a successful op," said Cade.

"That's not what I meant. How do we get out of here now? We're in the middle of the park. I don't think I can fight my way out of here again," said Sepia.

"We have a ride," said Cade. He pressed a small box on his side and a blinking light began to go off.

"It's a throwback but it doesn't seem to be affected by the EMP field," said Cade as he looked up to the sky. As he scanned the horizon, Sepia sat on the ground, outside the charred circle and took a deep breath.

"Over there--there she is," said a voice.

Sepia jumped to her feet, guns drawn and immediately regretted doing so. Turning in the direction of the voice, she faced Xavier carrying an injured Lisa and followed by Red Jen.

"X, what happened? Is she okay?" Cade said as he ran over to Xavier.

"After we were ambushed, some Unholy attacked us. I'm just glad it wasn't nighttime. Then in the middle of the fight she got hit by some lightning or energy that took them out, but left her like this."

Cade turned to a battered Red Jen.

"What happened to you? Your last transmission had your gunman down and you were going hunting," said Cade.

"They dissolved the ward stone and killed Chuck. I found them and ended them. I was making my way out of the park to the rendezvous point when I got hit by that same thing. Next thing I know he's over me yelling in my face," said Jen as she pointed at Xavier.

"She was out cold, you should have seen her. I thought she was gone," said Xavier.

"Where is your sword, rookie?" said Jen looking at Sepia.

Sepia and Cade looked at each other. Cade looked at Jen.

"It was changed in her fight with that Nightmare thing. She has it, just not the same way," said Cade.

"You lost your sword? How could you lose a named blade?" said Jen.

"Jen, give it a rest. I told you she has it and so she has it. Let it be," Cade said as he stood between them.

Jen backed off and went to sit by a tree, mumbling to herself about incompetent hunters.

"I can see she still likes me," said Sepia.

"It's been a rough day all around," said Cade.

"Agreed, after this I could use a vacation. Will I get one? No, I will not," said Xavier.

Xavier laid Lisa down on the ground next to Sepia.

"Hey, you okay? You look like shit," said Xavier.

"Thanks. I could say the same thing about you," said Sepia.

"And you would be right. Cade, we planning on staying here or can I get my ass home?" said Xavier.

Above them as if on cue Sepia saw the modified Order helicopter.

"Let's make this quick, people!" said Bear.

"I thought they couldn't bring that thing in here with the EMP field?" said Sepia.

"Hep did something to it after reading that book --said it should make it possible to stay in here much longer without damaging the electrical components. Something about warding the bird and making it invisible to the EMP field," said Cade.

"What?" said Sepia.

"You can ask him when we get back. Let's get out of here," said Cade.

They boarded the helicopter and took off. Sepia could feel the wards around her as they rose, enclosing the park.

****

Several hours later as night fell a figure emerged from the trees near the remains of the last ward stone. It was a well-dressed man with a chimera tattoo on his neck. Behind him trailed several Brutes.

"Gather his body-- all of it --and bring it. Our lord would be most displeased if you left something behind," said the man.

"Yes, master," said the Brutes.

They gathered the head and body of Chimera and headed off into the night.

TWENTY-SIX

"YOU CAN'T STAY HERE NOW. I gave them my word," said Gan.

"I know, Gan. How long do I have to stay with them?" said Sepia.

"Until they say otherwise, and until you are ready," said Gan. His voice softened somewhat and he placed a hand on her shoulder.

"I know you're worried about the dispensation. Let me worry about that, blueberry. Anna and I have a lot of history. You have a few days to say your goodbyes. It will be better if you go to them rather than have Anna come get you, trust me on this," he said.

"I know, I just don't like it. Anna and I didn't exactly hit it off," said Sepia.

"She isn't what I would call, friendly. It's for the best. The threat from the park is neutralized for now, though that doesn't mean Marks is going to stop. You are still blacklisted and now there are hunters that are stronger than before. We still don't know what this failsafe is or how it will affect you," said Gan. "It will be good for you to lay low for a while."

"I need to go see Hep. Will I be able to visit you or Cade?"

"When Anna says you're ready, then yes, if I haven't convinced her to not kill me by then, it may be a little difficult. Let's cross that bridge when we get there," said Gan.

Sepia hugged Gan. "I'm going to miss you, old man."

"It's not forever, Blue, and I still have a few cards to play. I'm not done yet. Now get going," said Gan.

Sepia left the conference room and looked for Cade. She found him in the armory with Hep.

"Sepia, we were just discussing the effect warding can have on weapons in proximity to the park," said Cade.

"Hi Cade, Hep," said Sepia.

"Gan told you. How long do you have?" said Cade.

"A few days, but I know the Sisters. I'd better not drag this out any longer," said Sepia.

"You're right. Anna is not known to be patient," said Hep. He handed Sepia the ward book covered with the cloth, and a large manila envelope.

"Thank you for everything, Hep. We couldn't have done this without your help," said Sepia.

Hep waved his hand, dismissing her comment. "You guys did all the work. Here take this," he said as he handed her a blade he had inscribed with wards.

"Thank you," said Sepia.

"The wards make it almost unbreakable and you should be able to locate it wherever it is. Cade told me about your sword. Could I...see it before you go?"

Sepia took the blade and placed it in a thigh sheath. She took a step back and extended an arm, materializing her blade.

"I never get tired of that," said Cade.

The sword had no trace of black, but a green energy ran up and down its length. The inscription remained the same.

Hep whistled low as Sepia handed the blade to him.

"It's the same and yet different. It feels much stronger somehow," said Hep.

He walked over to one of his anvils and sliced downward. The blade cut through the metal easily, shearing off a piece.

"Yes, definitely stronger. I'm sure it can do much more in your hands, Sepia. I will look into it but there isn't much documentation about named blades and their properties," said Hep.

"Thank you, Hep," said Sepia. She took back the blade and it flowed into her hand like liquid mercury and disappeared, absorbed into her skin.

"That is amazing," said Hep.

Sepia turned to Cade who was assembling a rifle and adjusting the sight. He ran his hand through his hair and smiled at Sepia. It was a sad smile.

"Who were you assigned to?" said Sepia.

"I'm with Jen. Gan said it was a good match and you not being a hunter..." his voice trailed off.

"No, it's a good match. You're the best gunman out there and she's a good hunter. One of the best, even if she hates my guts," said Sepia. She managed to say the words without choking up.

"She may be one of the best, but in my book you're the best, Blue," said Cade. She gave him a hug.

"You take care of yourself and watch your hunter," said Sepia.

"You too, Blue. I'll see you soon, right?"

"Probably sooner than you think," said Sepia.

She walked out of the armory with her bag and the ward book. She left Grey Command into the bright morning sun. Outside was a large SUV and Asha stepped out.

"Hello, Sepia. Good to see you again," she said.

"Hello, Asha," said Sepia. She stepped into the SUV and looked back one last time. She was leaving everything she knew behind.

She took a deep breath and let it out. "I'm ready," she said to Asha.

"Not yet you aren't, but you will be," said Asha with a smile.

The End

Thank you for reading Sepia Blue-Rise of the Night. I truly hope you enjoyed reading it as much as I enjoyed writing it. If you enjoyed this story please consider getting The Last Dance- A Sepia Blue Short. There you can find out a bit more about Sepia's history. Thank you for joining me, please share with family and friends. It would be great if you could leave me a review at Amazon or wherever you purchased the story. Thank you, your reviews help!

Please visit my blog, leave a comment and join my email list.

I look forward to hearing from you.

Other titles by Orlando Sanchez

The Spiritual Warriors

Blur-A John Kane Novel

The Deepest Cut-A Blur Short

The Last Dance A Sepia Blue Short

Connect with me online:

Blog: http://nascentnovels.com/

Facebook

https://www.facebook.com/OSanchezAuthor

Twitter: https://twitter.com/SenseiOrlando

About the Author:

Author Orlando Sanchez has been writing ever since his teens when he was immersed in playing Dungeon and Dragons with his friends every weekend. An avid reader, his influences are too numerous to list here.

Aside from writing, his passion is the martial arts; he currently holds a 2nd Dan and 3rd Dan in two styles of Karate. If not training, he is studying some aspect of the martial arts or martial arts philosophy, or writing in his blog. For more information on the dojo he trains at, please visit www.mkdkarate.com

Made in the USA
Monee, IL
28 June 2022